The Adventures of Tom Leigh

The Adventures of
TOM LEIGH

Phyllis Bentley

Illustrated by Burt Silverman

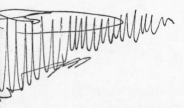

DOUBLEDAY & COMPANY, INC.   GARDEN CITY, NEW YORK

LIBRARY OF CONGRESS CATALOG CARD NUMBER 66–12175
ILLUSTRATIONS COPYRIGHT © 1966 BY DOUBLEDAY & COMPANY, INC.
TEXT COPYRIGHT © 1964 BY PHYLLIS BENTLEY
ALL RIGHTS RESERVED
PRINTED IN THE UNITED STATES OF AMERICA
FIRST EDITION IN THE UNITED STATES OF AMERICA

Contents

The Adventures of Tom Leigh

1 · I Come to Yorkshire

M<small>R.</small> DANIEL DEFOE, the famous author of *Robinson Crusoe* and my very good friend, has told me in a letter that I should be wise to write down all that happened to me in the matter of the stealing of the cloth from my master, Mr. Firth, so that I may be able to give a very clear and exact account of all those strange events. I shall be the chief witness against the thieves, he says, when the trial takes place at York assizes, and the whole West Riding of Yorkshire will have its eyes on me, for not only Mr. Firth, but several other clothmakers have had cloth stolen, they think by these same men. It is a great responsibility for a lad of fourteen, says Mr. Defoe (I was born in the year of Our Lord 1708). Indeed I feel it so. I only hope my broken arm, which I took in the fight, will have healed by then, for I feel foolish wearing it in a kind of sash. But when I said this to Mr. Firth, he laughed.

"Nay, Tom," he said, "a wound bound up makes a lad look a hero."

"I am not a hero, Mr. Firth," said I, embarrassed.

"That is for others to say, Tom," said he, laughing again. "Not you."

I had shown Mr. Firth Mr. Defoe's letter of course, and he approved what Mr. Defoe advised me about writing down all my recollections of the affair, and has set me down here with ink and paper and several pens (sharpened for me by Gracie) and told me to write every day until I have finished my story, and not to trouble myself about my work at the loom. I asked him where he thought I should begin the tale. At this he looked very serious.

"Why, Tom," he said soberly, "I think you had best begin with your first coming to Yorkshire. For there is a matter or two there which is not cleared up, you know. Your father's watch, for instance. And that voice you say you heard."

"I heard the voice, sir," I said obstinately.

"Aye, so you say. Remember, Tom," said Mr. Firth, laying his hand very kindly on my shoulder: "In court you will be on your oath. Everything you say must be the truth, the whole truth, and nothing but the truth. So you had better write in the same way."

"I will write the truth, Mr. Firth," said I.

I spoke rather sharply, and looked him straight in the eye, for I was tired of being doubted, knowing what pain any suspicion of my honesty would have given my father. However, I thought his advice was sound, and so I begin with a short account of my life in Suffolk with my father.

My name is Thomas Leigh, as was my father's. He was a good weaver, the best in all the countryside round Lavenham, a town noted for centuries for its fine cloth. My grandfather was by name Thomas Leigh again, and my great-grandfather too; he was also a weaver, and one of good repute, but he was noted throughout the county for another cause, namely that being a man of great strength and courage, he halted the horses of a coach carrying the daughter of a noted Earl de Vere which were running away through Lavenham, and this Earl, in gratitude for the saving of his daughter's life, presented my great-grandfather with a silver watch. On the back of this watch outside were engraved his initials, T.L., and on the inside was engraved *December 16th, 1660,* this being the date when the horses bolted. This watch came in course of time to be inherited by my father, and you can imagine that he was very proud of it and cherished it, though it no longer told the time. He had it with him, on his person, when we came north to Yorkshire, and that I swear.

My father, though a tall man and sinewy like his famous forebear and not lacking in any way in courage, was rather quiet and sober in manner. It seems my mother died when I was born, and he lost his merriment from that day. But he was the kindest and best of fathers to me; he never said a harsh word to me, and would play and talk with me when we were alone together in our cottage, and always saw that I had the best food we could afford, and paid for me to go to the little school in our part of the town. He was much respected in Lavenham, not only for his great skill at the loom but also for his calm judgment and straightforward honesty. So that when he decided to accept Mr. Somebody's offer of very good wages to go north to Yorkshire and teach his weavers there how to make really fine cloth instead of the coarse stuff they wove, it seemed to me the right thing to do, and certainly many of the Lavenham weavers envied him.

I say Mr. Somebody because this was one of the difficulties of my situation later; I did not know his name although I saw him when he came to visit my father. I did not much care for what I saw, though he wore a handsome suit of cinnamon cloth, for he was a short stout man with turned-out toes and prominent eyes, who held his head very far back as if to look at his own nose, and flipped his thumb-nails against each other when he was in any way vexed. When I ran in from play and found him talking to my father, he frowned a little and flipped his nails thus, and looked over my head when my father spoke of me as his son who would accompany him to Yorkshire.

"There is no need to mention my name to your son," he said. "Keep it altogether to yourself, if you please. Both here and in Yorkshire it will be best to keep our business private."

So my father never mentioned his new master's name. What there might be in Yorkshire to make this secrecy desirable, I did not then know, but I guessed, rightly as it proved, that it was intended to gain a business advantage over rivals by springing on the market finer cloth than they could weave. My father explained to me why secrecy might be good in Lavenham. It seemed that while some people thought the cloth trade was slowly dying in Lavenham, others opposed this view and thought it wrong of my father to leave, and the farmers might have refused to sell their wool to this northern clothier next time he came round, if they had known him.

My father always said I resembled my mother in face and disposition. As to face I cannot say, but I have heard that she was lighthearted and gay, and certainly before all this happened I was a merry enough lad. In appearance I take after my father, being now well grown for my age, not broad but sinewy, with dark hair and eyes and an even color in my cheeks.

So we sold our goods and left Lavenham. It was a bright spring morning when we said good-by to it, and I shall never forget how black and white the timbered weavers' cottages looked in the sunshine, and the great square gray flint steeple of our church towering over all. My father looked back rather mournfully, I thought, as we left Water Street, but I felt eager for the adventure of a new life. So we set off, with our few clothes and goods on our backs.

I do not remember how many days we took to reach Yorkshire. They were very happy days; the weather held good, sunny but not too warm, with scarcely any wind. My father had money in his pocket, five gold guineas and a handful of silver, from our sale, and as he was going to good employment he did not scruple to put up in an inn each night and buy us a good supper and a good breakfast, with bread and cheese which we ate by the side of the road for our midday meal. So we journeyed along pleasantly enough, enjoying the sights of the road.

Then we came to Yorkshire—to the West Riding of Yorkshire, I should say, for it seems there are several parts of this large county.

From the first I was daunted by the landscape, for I had never seen anything like it before. In Suffolk we had a few pleasant hills, smooth and nicely rounded and not too high, with plowed land and green pastures rolling gently to their summits. But these Pennine hills were terrible affairs! High and rough and steep, dark at the top, sometimes rocky, and coming on and on, one after the other, folding into each other so that you could never see the end of them, and as fast as you climbed one you had to go down from it into a valley, and then up again to another hill—well, they were more like mountains. Streams tumbled headlong down from them, dashing over rocky beds. The fields were all divided by stone walls instead of hedges, and there was scarcely a strip of plowland to be seen. The lanes were steep and stony, except that sometimes there would be a kind of narrow stone platform running along one side, above the level of the rest; we learned this was called a causey. My father seemed troubled by these causeys; I could not quite see why.

"It seems to me they are built to keep passers-by out of the water," he said when I asked him. "It seems as if much water might pour down these steep lanes."

He looked apprehensively up at the sky as he spoke. And well he might; for the weather had broken. Gray clouds were flying across the sky, driven by the strongest winds

I had ever known, coming always roaring from the west. Soon we were spattered by large cold drops of rain, which presently became longer and longer showers, and as the afternoon waned these showers turned to heavy pouring rain, which seemed to drive into our faces whichever way we turned, so that soon we were drenched. To add to our miseries we were lost. The lanes hereabouts did not keep to the valleys so that you could judge your course by the river, but wandered about halfway up the hills where there seemed to be level stretches on which stood houses at a distance from each other, not snug cozy villages as in Suffolk. There were no men working in the fields from whom to ask the way, and we hesitated to go down the side lanes to the farms, in case we should be ill received by their dogs. Besides, to tell you the truth, the speech of these Yorkshire folk, when we did occasionally encounter one, was so outlandish to our ears that we hardly understood what they said. (Now, of course, I have grown used to it and understand it well; I can even speak a word or two of this dialect myself.)

We had climbed a steep hill and were tired and soaked to the skin as we walked slowly along a road, level for once, when we saw opening before us a sharp drop, worse than the one we had just climbed. We both gave a kind of groan and halted.

"We'll go into this inn," said my father.

For a few paces ahead another lane joined ours, and at the side stood an inn, the Fleece it was called. This seemed a comfortable kind of name connected with our trade, such as we had often seen above inns in Suffolk, so we thankfully entered.

It was a tremendous relief to be out of the wind and rain, but oddly enough I felt wetter than ever, and ashamed

of my hair streaming down my back, and my soaked clothes
which now began to steam. The inn parlor was crowded
with men drinking and talking, and the landlord in his shirt
sleeves behind the bar did not at first notice us, and gave
us a rather unfriendly glance when he did. My father asked
the way to Halifax.

"Halifax! You're five miles off," said the landlord. "Up and down miles, too. Where've you come from, then?"

"Lavenham."

"Never heard of it. I thought you were foreigners, from the start."

"You can sell us some ale, however? The boy is chilled to the bone."

"Have you the money to pay for it, eh?"

"Surely!" exclaimed my father. He flushed angrily, and put his hand toward the breast of his jacket, where the bag with his money lay.

"Oh, in that case," said the landlord, who followed this gesture with his shrewd little eyes: "Sit you down by t'fire and warm you. You mun be fair starved. I'll bring you summat to eat as well as drink, eh?"

My father thanked him, and we were soon sitting on the tall settle by the hearth, with a smoking dish of ham and eggs before us. Unfortunately—and it was indeed a true misfortune—the sudden warmth after the long miles of cold and rain had turned me sleepy. I did not see any of the faces around me as I ate, only a confused blur of mugs and hands and neckcloths through the smoke. My head was down on the table when my father shook me awake. With his other hand he was replacing his moneybag in its inner pocket. A discussion was going on as to the way he should take to Halifax. The landlord gave some directions which, though no doubt clear enough to him, sounded muddled and incomprehensible to us.

"He'd do best to go down Mearclough, by t'beck," offered a voice from the back of the room.

"Aye, well, happen he had. It'd be gainest, choose how," said another.

"Nay, it's coming dark. Best stick to t'lane."

"He'll never find it."

"One of you can set him on t'road."

"Nay, lad! It's all of a mile, and rain's fair teeming down."

"He's right out of his way."

"He should never have come here in t'first place."

I remember what they said very well, though at the time I did not understand it. Now I know that a *beck* is a stream, a *clough* the cleft in the hills down which it runs, *teeming* means pouring, and *gainest* means quickest, fastest. I was still half asleep when my father steered me out into the rain and set off briskly along the hill.

"Couldn't we stay the night at the inn, father?" I besought him, for my left heel had a blister and I was tired out.

"No."

"Why not?"

"I didn't much care for the look of some of the men in there," said my father, lowering his voice. "I wish I hadn't shown 'em my bag. Besides, we must be in Halifax market tomorrow morning."

We both quickened our steps. When we entered the inn it had been twilight, now it was dusk; the great hills loomed somberly around us, the wind roared, sleet was now mingled with the heavy rain.

"This is the way," said my father, turning off into a muddy path which dipped down steeply from the lane. "This will be the clough they spoke of."

It seemed to me a fearsome place. True, on our right there was one of those stone walls with which this county abounded, and a few straggling hawthorns, which gave us some shelter; but on our left at the bottom of a kind of narrow gorge a stream flung itself furiously downhill over a bed of rocks, with a clamor which almost overtopped the roar of the wind. The path was very muddy and slippery, and occasionally a sharp point of rock tripped me up. Once I was thrown sprawling; I thought I should fall into the stream but managed to cling to some very long tough grass halfway down the bank, and my father gave me a hand to climb up again.

It was now quite dark, or perhaps it seemed so because we came into a thicker belt of hawthorns; at any rate I could see nothing, not even my father just in front of me, so when he stopped suddenly I stumbled into him.

"Wait here a moment, Tom," he said in a troubled tone. "I am not sure of the way. There seems to be a bend here in the path."

I was not sorry to stand for a moment and catch my breath. Behind the wind, the rain, the roar of the stream, the slow heavy steps of my father as he edged his way along, I thought I heard a crackle behind the wall. But I had hardly had time to think what it might be—a footstep perhaps on broken twigs—before a voice pealed out, it seemed almost in my ear:

"Keep to your left!"

I swear I heard this, whatever Mr. Firth and Sir Henry and the Constable may say. It was a shout: loud, urgent, commanding, and at the same time a shout of warning. Then there came a wild high scream and a sound, difficult to describe but clear enough in what it meant, of a body falling over rocks.

"Tom!" cried my father. "Keep away, boy! Keep back! I'm—"

I rushed forward, and pitched straight down the bank, for the path took a bend to the right there, as my father had guessed. My father lay half amid rocks, half in a deep cold pool. I cried: "Father! Father!" and pulled at his arm, but he did not speak or stir. Then I felt his face, and it was under water, and I got my hands into his armpits and hauled at his shoulders frantically, and I kneeled in the water at the edge of the pool and got his head up on my knees and held him and tried to drag him out of the water, but he was too heavy for me to move. Indeed it was as much as I could do to hold him there, and gradually his body slipped down and his head fell forward, and just as I was beginning to feel that my aching arms could hold him no longer something fell heavily on the back of my head, and I knew no more.

2 In the Poorhouse

WHEN I CAME TO MYSELF I was lying in a very clean bed in a small room with a peaked roof and one very small window. I had never seen the room before, and after a time, as my senses cleared, I began to wonder where I could be. I sat up, but at once my head swam; I felt giddy and had to lie down again. The coverlet, I noticed, was a piece of undyed white cloth of the cheap rough kind called kersey, with several very bad faults in the weaving of it. Presently I made another attempt to rouse myself, and after one or two efforts managed to get out of bed and stumble to the window. A kind of despair seized me as I looked out. All round the horizon the hills rose and fell; the nearer ones were green with dark tops, the farther ones blue, for it was a sunny morning and this window was high and had a distant view. So I could not be in Suffolk. Then I remembered the bleak night and the tumbling stream and the weight of my father's body and the strange slack feel of his cheek against mine, and I tore the coverlet off the bed and wrapped myself in it and pulled open the door of the room—and fell straight into the arms of an enormous fat woman with very red cheeks, who was coming in with a mug of gruel in her hand.

"What are you about, you daft lad?" she said in that cheerful railing Yorkshire tone which I have now learned is not meant to be unfriendly. "Do you want to kill yourself? Get back into bed and sup your gruel."

I did as I was told, for I hardly had strength to do

aught else, but I demanded: "Where am I?" in an urgent tone.

"Where are you? In Barseland poorhouse, to be sure. Where did you think you were?"

"Poorhouse?" I exclaimed in horror. "What am I doing in a poorhouse? What will my father say? I must leave at once."

"Now, don't fret yourself, love," said the fat woman, pressing her hand kindly on my shoulder. "It's no use leaving here till tha's somewhere else to go, tha knows."

"Where is my father?"

"Well—he's not in Barseland, and that's a fact."

"Where is Barseland? Is it near Halifax?"

"Aye, it is."

"Then I'll go to Halifax. My father will be there."

The fat woman stepped to the door, and called out: "Mr. Gledhill! Mr. Gledhill!"

After a moment a tall, thin, serious-looking man with a very long face and gray hair came into the room.

"This is Mr. Gledhill, the Barseland Constable and Overseer of the Poor," said the fat woman to me. "So answer him as straight as you can. He's asking for his father," she said to Mr. Gledhill.

Mr. Gledhill looked graver than ever.

"What is your name, my boy?"

"Thomas Leigh. Most people call me Tom."

"How old are you?"

"Fourteen."

"You were with your father, were you? What were you doing down Mearclough on such a wild stormy night? Where had you come from? Where were you going to? Those are a lot of questions; take your time and answer as fully as you can."

I told him all about our home at Lavenham, and why we

had come to Yorkshire, and how we had lost ourselves, and the scene at the inn, and the voice that had sent my father stumbling down the bank—at this he and the fat woman exchanged looks of disbelief, which vexed me. But on the whole he seemed pleased, I thought, with my account.

"Your father had a trade, then?"

"Of course! He's a weaver. A very *good* weaver."

"Not a vagrant, then," said the fat woman.

"Seems not," said Mr. Gledhill.

"What is a vagrant?" I asked.

"Somebody who wanders about the country without money—a man with no trade—a beggar."

"How dare you say my father is a beggar!" I shouted angrily.

"We just said he wasn't, love," said the fat woman. "Since he had a trade."

"He has a trade and he has money," I cried. "He has five guineas in gold and a handful of silver—well, nearly a handful," I corrected myself, remembering my father paying for our meat and drink at the Fleece. "I'll go to Halifax and find him, and then he'll explain it all to you."

"Listen, lad," said Mr. Gledhill. "I'm sorry to have to tell you this, my boy, but it must be done. You've lost your father, Tom. He broke his neck when he fell into the stream. He fell on the rocks, you know."

"Do you mean he's—dead?"

"Dead and buried," said the fat woman.

At this I fell into a kind of violent stormy shouting and weeping and beating my hands against the coverlet. The fat woman threw up her hands and left, but Mr. Gledhill drew up a chair and sat through it all in solemn silence. When from sheer exhaustion I quieted at last, he began to question me about my family in Lavenham. But I had no blood kin living anywhere, and so I told him. He stroked his chin thoughtfully.

"We shall have to send you back to Lavenham, Tom," he said. "You don't belong to Barseland, you've no settlement here, you see. We can't pay out Barseland money for a Lavenham pauper."

"I am not a pauper," I said indignantly. "My father had money with him. Surely that money is now mine?"

"Aye, it is. Or it would be if we could find it," said Mr. Gledhill. "Your father had no money on him when we found him. I examined him myself, Tom. There was no money."

"It was in a bag in an inner pocket of his jacket."

"There was no money, Tom."

"Then somebody stole it," I cried.

"Are you accusing me?" said Mr. Gledhill coldly.

"No, no. But the money was there."

"We found no money, we entered him in our records as a vagrant. At present you are a pauper and must stay in this poorhouse until you can be sent back to Lavenham. You are under the orders of Mrs. Hollas, whom you have seen, and her husband, who is the Master of this poorhouse. They will set you to work as soon as you are able. I hope you soon will be able, for we have kept you for a fortnight already."

"A fortnight?" said I, staggered.

"Aye, a fortnight. You have been ill of a fever. What with lying out all night in Barseland stream, with rain and wind beating on you, and the bang on your head, perhaps it is no wonder," said Mr. Gledhill.

His voice, which had turned so cold when I said my father's money had been stolen, seemed now to warm again, and I took courage.

"Mr. Gledhill, I accuse nobody, believe me I accuse nobody, but my father had money, just as I told you, it was in a calfskin bag. Maybe the bag fell into the pool? Please have a search made for it. Please, Mr. Gledhill!"

"Well—when the pool has dried a little in this fine weather, I will have it dragged. Meanwhile, you had best keep quiet about the money, Tom. If money has really been stolen from a dead man, it will be a bad lookout for Barseland. Happen the bag fell into the pool. Let us hope so. If, indeed, there was a bag at all."

"My father had a leather bag with five golden guineas in it," said I firmly.

Mr. Gledhill's face twitched with annoyance, and he rose and made to quit the room. At the door, however, he paused, and turned to me, saying:

"Try not to grieve, Tom. When you are recovered—" he hesitated, "when you are recovered I will take you to see your father's grave."

He went out. So there I was, of all boys, I thought, the most wretched. Fatherless, destitute, a pauper in a poorhouse in a strange land. I felt so lonely, so helpless, so desolate, that it was all I could do not to throw myself face down on my pillows and cry like a girl.

Since that time I have heard bad accounts of many poorhouses: how the inmates were ill fed and ill clothed, slept in dirty beds and were employed continually on hard exacting tasks. But except for the tasks, I did not find life too hard at the Barseland poorhouse. Mrs. Hollas, though bustling and rough in her manner and somewhat coarse in her speech, was kind at heart. Her husband I did not like so well. A thin wiry little man with red eyebrows, a very pale hollow face and strong freckles, he was mean in disposition, and I thought would have cheated Barseland and us if he had been able. But Mr. Gledhill in his quiet dour way delved into all the expenditure very closely and often. Before one of his visits Mr. Hollas was always in a bad temper, and took it out on the inmates, cuffing the younger and shouting at the older among us. Indeed he was too much given at all times to cuffing heads, boxing ears, and hitting our wrists with his bunch of keys; we were always happiest when he was away on one of his expeditions into the north of the county to buy provisions. It seemed that farther north in Yorkshire there was more fertile land than in our part of the West Riding, and Mr. Hollas had a cousin who lived up that way, in Skipton, and from him he bought cheese and sides of mutton for our benefit. At cheap rates, he said, and certainly I never heard Mr. Gledhill grumble overmuch about these prices when he and Mr. Hollas went into the barn together to check the purchases. Mr. Hollas was always agitated and fidgety as he unlocked the door, Mr. Gledhill very slow and quiet, with long bills in his hand.

Partly, therefore, owing to this useful cousin of Mr. Hollas, but more, I thought, to the watchfulness of Mr. Gledhill, our food, though neither ample nor varied, was sufficient; the cheese and oatmeal porridge and milk were plentiful, the meat, though not plentiful, was enough to give us all a small slice a day, and as the days went on I grew used to eating oatcake. At first these thin spongy ovals which were hung up on strings above the fire to dry filled me with dislike, but I soon found that when they were crisp their sharp taste and crackle were not disagreeable.

The poorhouse was kept clean, and we were given the chance to wash our linen. Though as regards clothes I was in evil case; our bundles had vanished with my father's money, so I had but one shirt, my shoes had dried out of shape and split, and my breeches were so torn and stained by my adventure in Barseland stream that I was ashamed to be seen in them.

There were only nine of us at that time in the poorhouse, five very old people, three young children and myself. Thus

I had no one of my own age to talk to, and this increased my feeling of being alone. However, I had not much time to think of this, for from morning till night I was busy with the tasks set me by Mr. and Mrs. Hollas. I ran errands in the sparse, bleak hillside village of Barseland, I washed floors and dishes, I peeled potatoes, turned the meat on the spit, chopped wood, cracked coal, harnessed the horse, Dobbin, in the cart for Mr. Hollas to go to Skipton, unloaded the sides of mutton he brought back.

One day when Mr. Gledhill came I was scrubbing the floor of the porch. He seemed vexed and, calling Mr. Hollas, told him sharply that he should be teaching me a trade.

"Let Lavenham teach him a trade," growled Hollas. "I have no time."

"When shall I go back to Lavenham, sir?" I asked.

"Tom, I have bad news for you, I fear," said Mr. Gledhill. "I have come to tell you that Lavenham will not accept you. They say your father gave up his settlement there. They say Halifax should take you and pay."

"And will Halifax do so?"

"I shall not even ask them," said Mr. Gledhill grimly. "We must apprentice you to some master here, a clothier or a collier. Your father was a weaver, you say."

"Yes, sir."

"Do you know aught of his trade?"

"My father taught me to card and spin as a child," I answered proudly, "and I have been learning to throw the shuttle on the loom for two years now."

"It had best be a clothier, then," said Mr. Gledhill. He looked me up and down distastefully, and said to Mr. Hollas: "We must find some better clothes for him before I take him to Sir Henry. If he's in rags nobody'll want him."

Mr. Hollas growled and grumbled. "We've no breeches here for a lad his size," he said.

"He's a good lad all t'same," said Mr. Gledhill, giving me a solemn smile. "I'll see if I can beg some breeches and a shirt or two for him in the village. His jacket's not too bad."

I hardly knew what to feel when Mr. Gledhill had left me. To leave the poorhouse would be a joy, a renewal of hope; but to wear clothes that had been begged for me was to be a pauper indeed. The worst thing of all was that saying *nobody'll want him*. It struck me hard that nobody in the wide world wanted me; from being the chief point of my father's life I had become a useless, unnecessary thing, a nuisance, something to be thrown away. This was hard to stomach.

Presently there came a day when Hollas told me Mr. Gledhill would fetch me next morning to go before the magistrate. Sir Henry Norton, he told me, was the Justice of the Peace for these parts; a widower he was, with one son. I rose early and washed myself all over and combed my hair and tidied my clothes as well as I could, for though my heart was in my shoes I was too proud to show it. While I was at my porridge, Mrs. Hollas—Mr. Hollas had set off on one of his excursions —called me to come to Mr. Gledhill. She was laughing and nodding and nudging me in the ribs, so I saw she meant there was some good news, but Mrs. Hollas' notion of good news would not be mine, I thought, so I went in quietly. But the news was really good, for there on the table lay some new clothes: a narrow gray cloth coat and a pair of breeches of the same stuff, a clean shirt, a blue-colored neckerchief, a pair of gray knitted stockings and some strong wooden clogs.

"These are for you, Tom Leigh," said Mr. Gledhill with one of his solemn smiles.

Suddenly, seeing them lying there, I felt how greatly I had hated slouching about in my stained rags, and I could hardly find my voice to speak my gratitude.

"Is it you I have to thank, sir, or Barseland?" I said in a stifled tone.

"Neither, Tom. The men who were at the Fleece Inn when you and your father called there that night have had a whip round to fit you out. It seems they feel themselves to blame that they didn't come out and set you on the right road."

"They *were* to blame!" I cried, but I stopped short, remembering the rain and how we were strangers. "But I thank them very heartily, all the same."

I dressed myself in my new clothes, with my shirt collar out over my jacket, and tied the blue neckerchief round my throat, and set off along the road beside Mr. Gledhill, to Sir Henry Norton's mansion. This was a very large old house, with fine tall chimneys and gables, and a double row of mullioned windows in the center. The house was of stone, as all West Riding houses seem to be, and there was no moat round it, such as you often see round such houses in Suffolk. But then, the hills in the West Riding are so steep and frequent—everything seems to be built halfway up a hill —that you do not have to dig moats to drain off the water; the rain pours down the hillsides in hundreds of streams, as well I knew.

"Wait here till you are fetched," said Mr. Gledhill, going into the house by the back door.

There was a kind of paved courtyard where I stood, and presently a groom brought out a lively little horse, ready saddled, and led him to the mounting block. Then a boy about my own age, very fair in complexion, with big gray eyes, and handsomely dressed in a black riding suit with well-polished boots, came out of the house and made to mount.

"You are late, Robert!" he cried to the groom, laughing.

"Now that I have a watch I shall expect you always on the hour."

He drew a watch out of his fob pocket and showed it to the groom, and they both laughed.

"I shall remember, Master Harry," said the groom.

It was such a pleasure to me to see a boy of my own age that I could not help drawing near to observe them, and suddenly I sprang forward and shouted:

"That is my father's watch!"

"What do you mean?" said Harry, his face reddening.

"Give it to me!" I jumped forward and tried to snatch the watch from Harry's hand, but the groom put out his arm between us.

"That is my father's watch!" I panted. "My father was murdered and his watch stolen!" (I had never used this word *murdered* before about my father's death, but now I was sure it had been so.)

"My father gave me this watch!" shouted Harry, jumping down and pushing the groom aside. "Are you calling my father a thief?"

"Somebody was a thief!" I cried.

I was about to explain how my father had been drowned when Harry hit me hard under the chin. Taken by surprise, I was felled to the ground. But I had been in fights before, at Lavenham; as Harry came for me I rolled aside, and got to my feet, and sprang at him and hit him hard in the face; he staggered back, for he was hampered by his hold on the watch, and we grappled and both fell to the ground together and rolled about, struggling to get free and strike each other. The horse danced in alarm, its hoofs clattering on the paving stones, and the groom yelled and we shouted at each other, and altogether there was a great noise and Sir Henry and Mr. Gledhill and two other gentlemen and a servingman ran out of the house to us. The servingman and Mr. Gled-

hill pulled Harry and me to our feet and parted us and we stood there rather hangdog, both our noses bleeding and our hair tousled and some buttons off. Mr. Gledhill dabbed at my nose with his handkerchief, for which I was grateful though I knew he was thinking only of my new shirt's safety.

"For shame, boys! What are you about? Harry, you should know better! Gledhill, I thought you said Tom Leigh was a quiet lad of peaceable disposition?"

"Disgraceful!" said Gledhill, giving me a shake.

"Nay, hold hard. Wait a minute," said Sir Henry. "Let us get to the root of this. Who was the first to strike?"

"Me," said Harry gruffly. "He said you were a thief, Father."

As sometimes happens when two boys who have been fighting are scolded by grown men, we began at once to feel more kindly to each other than to our elders.

"I did not mean to say you were a thief, Sir Henry," I said quickly. "Only this watch is my father's watch, it was given as a reward to my great-grandfather; my father had it in his pocket when he was killed in the stream. It does not go."

"Has he spoken of the watch before?" said Sir Henry to Mr. Gledhill.

"No, Sir Henry. Only of his father's guineas."

"Why have you not spoken of it before, boy?"

"I never thought of it," said I miserably.

"My boy," said Sir Henry, not unkindly, "I bought this watch a week ago in Bradford market. It is going well."

"It is my father's watch!" I cried, scarlet with rage and shame. A sudden thought struck me. "I can tell you what is engraved on it, inside."

"Give me the watch, Harry," said Sir Henry quietly. His son passed it over, still in its tortoise-shell cover. "Did you show the watch to Tom?"

"No, sir. He couldn't have seen it close, sir," said Harry with a sniff.

Sir Henry turned aside and drew out the watch, unseen by all.

"Well, boy?" he said.

"It has the letters *T.L.* and the date *December 16th, 1660*," said I triumphantly.

"I do not like this, Gledhill," said Sir Henry at last, turning round. "The inscription is as the lad says. Yet I bought the watch in Bradford market last Thursday. Has anyone from Barseland township journeyed to Bradford lately, do you know?"

"Not to my knowledge," said Mr. Gledhill, shaking his head.

"Well, I will inquire of the man who sold it to me, though I have known him long and he is reputable enough. Meanwhile, Harry, I fear I must take your watch from you lest it should be damaged and then prove to be not lawfully yours. I will keep it safely, Tom Leigh, until this doubt be cleared. Now, come all within, and let us finish this business of the apprenticeship. You two boys, shake hands, your enmity was founded on a mistake."

Harry offered me his hand frankly, and I took it, and we both grinned and I think he felt as friendly as I did.

"Shall I take Tom to clean up before he comes to court?" said Harry.

"Aye, you had best. He is not fit to appear before the law in that condition," said Sir Henry severely.

He moved away into the house, limping a little and leaning rather heavily on his cane. The rest of us followed, Harry and I of course coming in last.

Indoors, Harry touched me on the arm to show that I was to follow him, sprang away up the wide shallow staircase and led me along the passage to his bedchamber. I was amused and rather relieved to find that it lacked the neatness of which Sir Henry would have approved. Coats were strewn over the chairs, splashed riding boots stood beneath; a Latin grammar lay open, face downwards, in the hearth as if it had been thrown there in disgust, a whip leaned in a corner, and some gloves, handkerchiefs and neckcloths lay in a confused heap on the dressing table. I wandered to the windows. The room lay to the side of the house, and looked up over banks of bushes toward a steep hill.

"Here you are, Tom," said Harry, pulling me toward a washstand on which stood a handsome rose-patterned ewer and basin. "There's water in the jug; take off your jacket and have a good wash."

I was glad of the change and felt better when I had sluiced my face in the cold water.

"Hurry, now, or my father's temper will mount," said Harry.

He bustled me into my jacket and seized my arm and rushed me downstairs and along a narrow passage, and paused in front of a half-open door.

"Knock and go in," he said, giving me a push. "Good luck, Tom."

I entered soberly. The room, small and cold, was clearly kept for Sir Henry's business. It was very bare, furnished only with a big table drawn along one side, with two handsome carved chairs behind and some plainer ones set about the room. On the table lay writing materials and a pair of scissors. I did not presume to sit down, but stood by Mr. Gledhill. The other two gentlemen seated themselves at the side of the room.

"Well, come, Gledhill, begin. Make your application," said Sir Henry testily.

Mr. Gledhill stood up and gave my name and age and the tale of my coming to Yorkshire. It seemed to me they had all

heard it before and listened impatiently. While he droned
on I had leisure to look at them. Sir Henry was the first man
I had seen in Yorkshire wearing a full-bottomed wig—the
others all wore short cut wigs—so he appeared very dignified
and handsome; his face was lean and serious and his dark
eyes keen. I gazed at the other two men in trepidation, won-
dering which was to be my master. Their appearance was
very different: one a stocky, sturdy man with a round florid
face, big hands and a rather quick-tempered look about him;
the other pale and tight-lipped and dry.

"Are you willing to take Thomas Leigh as your bound
apprentice, Firth?" said Sir Henry.

To my great relief, the stocky florid man stood up; the
tight-lipped man must be the other Overseer of the Poor for
Barseland, Mr. Gledhill's colleague.

"Well—I'm a bit put out by his fighting, and that's a fact,
Sir Henry," said Mr. Firth. "He won't have to do no fighting
at my place, I warrant you."

"The lad is right enough; my son struck him first; any boy
with spirit would hit back. Come—yes or no?"

"Well," said Mr. Firth, fidgeting from one foot to the
other. "It's my wife, you see. An apprentice means more
cooking, like. And if she thinks he's a fighting cock, well!"

"Of course if you'd rather pay the ten-pound fine for re-
fusing," snapped the tight-lipped Overseer.

"I could do that without any help from you, John Swain!"
cried Mr. Firth, the hot color rushing into his face.

"There's a two-pound bounty," began the tight-lipped
man, but Sir Henry spoke over him, drowning his words.

"Now, Firth," he said, "I shall not talk about fines and
bounties. To a warm man like you they make little matter."

"That's right," muttered Mr. Firth, glancing angrily at the
Overseer.

"I shall ask you to think of the lad himself. Here he is, a

pauper through no fault of his own; no mother, his father dying strangely in our own township. He is friendless and alone. Suppose it was your Gracie in such a case."

"My Gracie will be well provided for."

"Let us hope so," said Sir Henry gravely.

"I'll take him if you don't want him," said the tight-lipped man.

For the life of me I could not help a start of anguish, and I gazed imploringly at Mr. Firth. I met his eyes, and it seemed to me he wavered.

"Well—" he began.

"He's a healthy lad and not ill-looking," put in Sir Henry.

"He can read and write and card—his father was a weaver, think on," said Mr. Gledhill.

"In that case I'll take him," said Mr. Firth.

It seemed to me, however, that my accomplishments were only an excuse, a reason for him to give his wife, which he was relieved to have; he took me really from mere warmth of heart, and perhaps a little to spite the tight-lipped Overseer.

"Thank you, sir," I said.

Mr. Firth snorted. "But no fighting," he said. "And no mention of fighting, lad. My wife wouldn't sleep in her bed if she thought you were a fighter."

I thought I saw a gleam of amusement pass between Sir Henry and Mr. Gledhill, and I wondered what Mrs. Firth could be like; but I kept my face very solemn and said: "No, sir," very respectfully.

"Have you prepared the indentures, Gledhill?" said Sir Henry. "Come, come, get them read; I can't be about this business all day. I've something else to think of."

A frown crossed his face as he spoke, and Mr. Swain burst out angrily:

"I've had cloth stolen from my tenters in the night."

"Nay! Never!" exclaimed Mr. Gledhill and Mr. Firth, looking very grave.

"Aye! A whole piece!"

"Well, come along, Gledhill, come along," said Sir Henry testily. "Get those indentures read, then we can discuss this wretched theft."

Mr. Gledhill drew out a large scroll of paper and unrolled it and read from the document. (I have Mr. Firth's part of the indenture here before me, so I can give the words exactly.)

" 'This Indenture made the twenty-third day of April in the Year of Our Lord 1722, between William Gledhill and John Swain, Churchwardens and Overseers of the Poor of the township of Barseland in the West Riding of the county of York, and Thomas Leigh, a poor child of the said township of the one part, and Stephen Firth of the same township of the other part; witnesseth, that the said Overseers of the Poor, with the consent of two of His Majesty's Justices of the Peace for the said Riding, put, placed and bound the said Thomas Leigh as an apprentice to and with the said Stephen Firth, with him to dwell and remain from the day of the date hereof, until the said apprentice shall attain the age of twenty-one years. During all which term the said apprentice well and truly shall serve, his secrets shall keep, his commands (being lawful and honest) at all times willingly shall perform, and in all things as a good and faithful servant shall demean himself toward his said master and all his family. And the said Stephen Firth—' "

"Wait a minute, Gledhill," said Sir Henry. "Do you understand all that, Tom? That is what you are promising to do."

"I understand, sir," I said. "But seven years seems a very long time."

"It is the law, Tom," said Sir Henry. "Go on, Gledhill.

Now, Tom, we'll hear what Mr. Firth promises to do for you."

"'And the said Stephen Firth,'" resumed Mr. Gledhill, holding the scroll well out in front of him and reading very loud and clear, "'doth promise to the said Overseers and his said apprentice, that he will educate and bring him up in an honest and lawful calling, to wit the mystery of a weaver—'"

He paused and looked at Mr. Firth, who nodded and said: "That's right."

"'—and in the fear of God. And that he will find, provide for, and allow unto his said apprentice sufficient, wholesome and competent meat, drink, washing, lodging, apparel and other necessaries meet for such an apprentice, during all the said term.'"

"Do you agree to that, Firth?" said Sir Henry, rather sternly.

"Aye, I agree," said Mr. Firth. He sighed ruefully and shook his head. "A lad like that'll be always eating, I shouldn't wonder."

"'And at the end of the said term—'"

"What, is there some more?" grumbled Mr. Firth.

"'—at the end of the said term he shall find, provide for, and deliver unto his said apprentice double apparel of all sorts—'"

"*Double* apparel! For heaven's sake," wailed Mr. Firth.

"'That is to say,'" boomed Mr. Gledhill, "'one good and new suit for the Lord's days, and another for the working days, of linen, woolen, hose, shoes, and all other necessaries meet for such an apprentice to have and wear.'"

"It's a costly business, is an apprentice," said Mr. Firth. "However, he's well clad at the start, that's something."

"He'll be very useful to you, both about the house and in the loom chamber," said Sir Henry.

Mr. Firth gave a subdued snort.

" 'In witness whereof, the said parties to these presents have hereunto interchangeably set their hands and seals the day and year above written.' "

"Is that all?" demanded Mr. Firth.

"Aye, that's all."

"Well, it's enough. Unless he was to take the whole of Upper High Royd, there isn't much more the indentures could give him."

"Now, Stephen," said Mr. Gledhill soothingly.

"Where do I sign?"

"Here and here."

The scroll was laid out on the table. Mr. Firth signed it twice, once halfway along its length, once at its foot. Then Mr. Gledhill and Mr. Swain signed twice, and then Sir Henry likewise signed twice.

"I have already obtained the necessary signatures from a second magistrate," he said.

"Do I not sign?" I asked. It seemed to me that when seven years of my life were being given away, I ought to sign the agreement myself.

"You cannot sign anything till you are twenty-one," said Mr. Swain shortly.

"Canst truly write, then, Tom?" said Mr. Firth, putting his hand on my shoulder.

"Yes, sir."

He gave me a smile and a kind of wink which seemed to say: *Don't take too much notice of all this to-do, we shall be well enough when we are alone together.* My heart warmed to him, and I smiled, though rather faintly, in reply.

"That's better," said he. "Cheer up! I cannot abide anyone sullen about me."

"Scissors, scissors, where are the scissors?" Sir Henry was saying impatiently.

"Here, sir," said I, picking them out from under the indentures.

He took them in his hand and to my amazement began to cut across the indentures at their halfway. He cut, too, in such a wavy, pointed, up and down kind of line, I was really horrified.

"Listen, Tom," said Sir Henry, smiling. "I cut these indentures like this so that only these two halves will fit into each other. The line where they are cut is *indented*, and that is how indentures get their name. Mr. Firth keeps one half and the Overseers keep the other half. So if either of them wanted to write new conditions and pretend they were the original ones, the other could say: 'Fit your paper into my paper.' If the papers did not fit, one of them was not the true one. Do you understand?"

"Yes, sir," I said, though I was astonished.

"Here is a leather apron, Tom, the sign that you are apprenticed; it is the gift of the Barseland magistrates. Put it on."

I tied the apron sadly round my waist.

"Well, that's all, I take it, Sir Henry? We can leave now, eh?" said Mr. Firth, rolling his half of the indenture and stuffing it in his pocket.

"Yes, that is all. Give me your hand, Firth. Now you give me yours, Tom Leigh. A good master and a good apprentice. I hope you will spend happy years together."

We both mumbled our thanks, feeling a trifle embarrassed, and then we were out of the house and in the April wind. A shower of light rain was falling softly to the earth.

"Spoiling the druft," said Mr. Firth crossly.

"Druft?" said I, perplexed.

"The drying of the cloth," said Mr. Firth, impatient.

We turned up a very steep, stony lane.

"The house is high on the hill?" I said.

"Well, it is called Upper High Royd, so you may guess," said Mr. Firth, laughing.

So I left the Barseland poorhouse, and began a new life as an apprentice.

3 The New Apprentice

WE CLIMBED STEADILY for some fifteen minutes. Suddenly Mr. Firth halted and cried out:

"What the hangment is Daisy doing down here?"

I looked at him in astonishment, for how he could describe the place where we stood as "down" I could not imagine. The hillside ahead of us sloped up steeply, to be sure, but all around us were hilltops, plunging sharply to valleys between. Nor did I perceive anyone to be referred to as Daisy at first, till hearing a loud "moo" nearby I looked over the wall and saw a brown and white cow. Mr. Firth leaned over the wall and rubbed her forehead, which she seemed to like.

"Canst drive a cow, Tom?" said he, laughing.

"Yes, sir, I think so," said I. I had never in fact driven a cow, but I had met them outside Lavenham, and I wanted to seem willing.

"Over the wall with you, then," said he. "And get her into that field up there and shut the gate. How it can have been left open passes my comprehension."

I climbed the wall—all the fields, as I have said, are divided by stone walls in the West Riding, not by hedges as in Suffolk—and approached Daisy. But giving me a reproachful look and moo she swung aside and stumbled off up the hill, so I had only to follow her.

I own I looked with great curiosity at Upper High Royd, as the house came into view round the fold of a hill. Mr. Firth had signed to a promise to teach me to be a weaver, so he must know that trade himself. But in Lavenham the weavers mostly lived in very small cottages, or sometimes just in one garret room. Upper High Royd was a solid stone-built house, old-fashioned in style, long and low with a stone porch and a couple of gables and rows of mullioned windows, and a barn and a small round building and a thresh-ing place across the end of the yard. Behind the house rose up a great stretch of moorland, a dark brown in color, with outcrops of rock, one very high rock in particular jutting out against the sky like a man's head. A beck—as they call their streams in this county—came tumbling down from this moor-land into a stone trough in the yard and then tumbled on again down the hillside. In front of the house there was a small sloping field, of oats I guessed, just showing green, and another small field of grass where Daisy was to pasture, al-ready occupied by a quiet brown mare; at the side, open fully to the sun, a long wooden fence stretched twenty yards or so. As I drew nearer I saw that it was not really a fence, for it had but two rows of bars across its uprights, one near the top, one near the bottom; besides, it seemed to stand by itself, its ends not touching any other fence or wall. I was perplexed about its use till I drew near and saw a man kneel-ing beside it, fastening the edge of a wet piece of blue cloth to a row of nails which stuck up along the top bar. I shut the gate on Daisy and approached, and stood watching while I waited for Mr. Firth. As the lane took a bend to avoid some of the steepness, while I had come straight up the fields, he would be a minute or two behind me. The wind blew strongly, but the shower was over and the sun was pleasant.

"Well?" said the kneeling man sharply, without turning. "Never seen a tenter before, lad?"

"Is that what they're called? No, I haven't," said I.

The man stood up and turned to me.

"Who are you, then?" he demanded. He was tall, very thin and stooping, wearing his own dark hair long and tied

back with a shabby dangling bow, and he had a sallow, bad-tempered, frowning face, with a pair of small, mean black eyes. I disliked his person and his face and his voice at once, and have not since changed my opinion. However, I answered politely.

"I'm Thomas Leigh, Mr. Firth's new apprentice," I said.

He started, and gave me a look of fury, his black eyes really sparkling with rage.

"In that case you can do some work," he snapped. "Get down on your knees and help me. Stretch the cloth down and fasten it like this."

He pulled the lower edge of the fastened part of the cloth down and fastened it on the lower row of nails (which bent downward) so that the fabric was stretched between the two bars. I knelt down and tried to do the same, but it was not easy, as the cloth had to be pulled upon quite heavily.

"Nay, take your coat off, or you'll soak your fine cuffs," he sneered.

I threw off my coat and turned up my sleeves and tried to pull the edge of the cloth onto the nails.

"You'll never make a clothier, that's plain," said he with a satisfied air as he watched my efforts.

He gave a sneering laugh and walked away beside the tenter, and continued attaching the cloth to the top row of nails. This action naturally jerked the whole length of the piece, so when the cloth ceased to move of course I noticed it and looked toward him. He was standing sideways to the tenter with his back toward me, waving his arms about above his head in most extraordinary gestures. I thought these gestures must have something to do with the cloth and the tenter, and watched carefully to learn them, so I was caught with my eyes on him when he dropped his arms and turned round.

"What are you staring at me for, you young spy?" he

cried in a rage, and he threw a few rough epithets at me with which I will not spoil this paper.

I was spared the necessity for a reply by the arrival of Mr. Firth.

"Now then, Jeremy!" he said. "No bad language either in house or tentercroft, if you please. This is Tom Leigh, my new apprentice."

"Aye, I've heard his name," said Jeremy in an angry tone. "You promised me, master, that you wouldn't take an apprentice."

"I did nowt o't'sort," replied Mr. Firth sharply. "I said I shouldn't take him unless he seemed a useful sort of lad."

"This lad'll never make a clothier."

"Why not? His father was a weaver."

"Missus will have something to say," muttered Jeremy.

"That's enough!" bawled Mr. Firth. "The boy's an orphan, and I've bound him apprentice, and that's that. This is Jeremy Oldfield, my journeyman weaver," he went on to me, dropping his voice to a more ordinary note. "You two will have to work together, so let me have no nonsense between you."

"Of course not, master," said Jeremy smoothly. "Pleased to meet you, Tom."

He offered his hand and I took it. It was cold and clammy, so that it sent a kind of shudder through me.

"Mr. Oldfield," I said, bowing my head.

"Oh, call me Jeremy, lad," said he in a sugary tone.

I said: "Jeremy," obediently, though it almost choked me.

"Father, Father, Father!" cried a voice, and a child came running out of the house toward us.

"My poppet, my darling," said Mr. Firth fondly, picking her up in his arms. "How have you done without Father this morning, love? Eh?"

"Mother says dinner is ready and you must come in," said the child.

Her face was now turned toward us, so I saw her clearly. She was a pretty enough little thing, about seven years old I thought, with a reddish-gold color of curly hair, very blue eyes and a very fair skin, like her father's. She had a merry smile, and over her left arm was draped a big sleek cat, of so exactly the same color as her hair that it was somehow comical. The cat, surprised and indignant no doubt at finding itself suddenly squashed between father and daughter, mewed and clawed for safety at what was nearest. This was Mr. Firth's arm, and he winced a trifle.

"Let Sandy down, love," he said, still in the same fond tone. The child released the cat's waist, and it sprang away in a hurry to the top of a wall, then suddenly paused and sat erect gazing round, as if we did not concern it in the least. "This is my little girl, Gracie, Tom," said Mr. Firth to me. "And you must always be very kind to her."

"Yes, sir," said I.

But Gracie scowled at me.

"Is he to live with us?" she asked.

"Yes, love."

"Will he be like Jeremy?"

"Aye, I suppose in a way he will."

Gracie buried her face in her father's shoulder and seemed to whisper to him, something probably adverse to me, for he colored a little.

"Well, well, never mind, we shall see, we shall all do well enough together, I doubt not. Come in now, lads; dinner."

"I can't leave the tentering, master," said Jeremy in a sanctimonious tone.

"Well, come in as soon as you've done," said Mr. Firth comfortably. "Come along, Tom."

I thought Jeremy had expected I would be told to stay

and help him, for his eyes had a gleam of hatred toward me; but Mr. Firth pushed me in front of him toward the trough.

"Best clean yourself up a bit, Tom," he said. "Mrs. Firth is very particular about being clean at table."

I washed myself at the trough, and Gracie danced out with a towel for me, and I went into the house feeling neat enough but ill at ease. The doorway went straight into a big room, the housebody they called it, with a long table and plenty of chairs and a big meal-ark and a tall clock in the corner and a huge coal fire blazing up the broad chimney, and a hearthrug of colored bits of cloth in front of it, on which lay Sandy the cat washing himself. A broad staircase rose up at one side. The table was set for a meal, with a big jug of ale in the center and a plate piled with crisp oatcake, and Mrs. Firth was taking a pie out of the oven, with a rough brown oven cloth in her hand.

"Margaret, this is Tom Leigh, our new apprentice," said Mr. Firth.

Mrs. Firth put the pie carefully on the table and then looked sideways at me.

"He's big for his age," she said disapprovingly.

She was tall and thin, with very fair hair rather tightly dressed under a stiff cap, and blue eyes like Gracie's only a little paler. A few years ago she had been a pretty woman, I thought, but now her lips were rather too tightly closed, and she had an air, not exactly peevish or petulant, but rather as though she thought herself superior to being a clothier's wife and found its tasks too heavy for her. For all that, I thought, she was a woman of good principle, who would do her duty if it killed her and however uncomfortable it might make those around.

"He'll be handy for fetching coals and water for you, Meg," said Mr. Firth in an apologetic tone.

"He'll eat his weight in meat, I'll be bound," said Mrs. Firth in her rather prim speech, tossing her head.

"Your father has apprentices, Meg," said Mr. Firth.

"Yes, but not from the poorhouse. From good respectable families we all know."

"Well, give the lad a chance," said Mr. Firth.

We sat down at table and Gracie said a childish grace. The pie was delicious, and a loaf of bread we ate with it was crisp and new. Mr. Firth asked me if I would have a second helping, but I declined though I could well have eaten it, fearing to appear greedy after what Mrs. Firth had said.

"I'm sorry you don't care for my pie, Tom Leigh," said Mrs. Firth, again tossing her head.

"I don't wish to eat more than my share," I blurted.

"Foolish boy! Pass up your plate," said Mrs. Firth severely.

Jeremy came in and ate very heartily, though not in a very elegant style. I marveled he did not see how much Mrs. Firth disliked his manners, for she kept primming her mouth and looking away from him.

When the meal was over Mr. Firth took me upstairs to the workshop.

This was a big room, with two looms standing side by side beneath a long row of windows. Two or three loom beams, long round balks of timber, leaned empty in one corner; in another lay a great sack of wool. A couple of very old pieces of cloth, the sort you use to cover the loom when you stop work on Saturdays, had been tossed into a third corner. A peg board for warping stood by the wall opposite the looms, and on a table nearby stood a neat pile of straw spindles full of yarn. At one end of the room was a big double door, going right down to the level of the floor; as we drew near it Jeremy suddenly skipped ahead and threw the leaves wide. I stepped back, startled, for another couple of steps forward would have taken me right out into the air. Mr. Firth was vexed.

"Be careful, Jeremy," he said. "We don't want the lad to take a tumble."

"No, indeed, Mr. Firth," agreed Jeremy; but his eyes glittered with malice so that I felt he would have been only too pleased to see me fall.

"What are the doors for?" I asked.

"It's a taking-in place," said Mr. Firth carelessly. "Now, Jeremy, you show Tom round and then let him help you; or you can put him to carding. I'm going to weave."

He spoke like a man who withdrew from vexations to a loved craft, and so it proved. He sat down at one of the looms and began to work the treadles and throw the shuttle from side to side—at least "throw" is the word they use for this action; it is really more like sliding. I watched him for a moment or two; the cloth grew rapidly. Mr. Firth with his quick temper might be a trifle uncertain in everyday life, I thought, but he knows cloth, he weaves evenly and well.

The other loom was empty; probably the piece of cloth now drying on the tenters had been woven there. Jeremy set to work warping, that is getting the yarn on to the beam in the loom, for a fresh piece of cloth.

This warping is such a difficult and complicated business to explain, though simple enough to do when you know how, that I most earnestly hope I do not have to explain it in court. I do not really see why I should have to do so, as it does not concern the story of the thefts, except that from the moment I began to turn the beam handle for Jeremy as he stood ready with the loops of yarn over his left arm, it was settled for good that I should get no fair dealing from him. For I had often done this for my father, and knew just how it should be done, so there was no reason for Jeremy to be continually "calling" me, as they say here when they mean scolding. He complained that I stood in his light, that my feet were in the way, that I turned the handle before he was ready and too quick and too sudden and too late—in fact, everything I did was wrong. My heart swelled as I listened to him; I thought: Seven years of this! However, presently Mr. Firth rescued me, saying irritably:

"Put him to carding, Jeremy, if he frames so ill."

Carding is fairly hard work but not unpleasant. A pair of cards is something between a pair of hairbrushes and a pair of wooden hands for patting butter into shape; each card is flat and square, with a flat handle off one side, and covered all over with little metal bristles. You put a lump of wool, a lump of sheep's fleece, onto one card, and then you draw it off with the other card, and so back and forth until what has been a curly, yellowish fleece turns into a soft white flat tissue. It is always a pleasure to me to see this happen. When the wool is all soft and white like this it is ready for spinning into yarn. It is an odd and amusing thing about clothmaking, as my father used to say to me; you go from breadth to length and then from length to breadth. The fleece, broad across the sheep's back, has to be turned into a long fine thread of yarn, and then many threads of yarn have to be woven together to make a broad piece of cloth. This wool had been dyed blue; it was a cheerful color and made a bright tissue. I got on well enough at carding, for I had done it before; Mr. Firth looked at my work himself, and approved it, so Jeremy could not complain.

All the same, the afternoon seemed terribly long; I was most truly thankful when at last the light began to dim a little, and Mr. Firth stopped work. The evening passed drearily enough; we ate a good supper; then Mrs. Firth went upstairs to put Gracie to bed, and Jeremy slipped out while she was absent; Mr. Firth sat smoking a long white pipe and reading a newspaper, and I sat hunched in a chair far from the fire, trying not to go to sleep. It grew dark, Mrs. Firth returned and lit the candles and began to knit a stocking.

"Shall I go out and fetch the cloth in from the tenter, master?" I said timidly, wishing to show myself willing for any task.

"Fetch piece in? Nay, lad, it'll not be dry yet," said Mr. Firth. "Druft was poor today—not much wind."

"You mean you'll leave it out all night?" said I, astonished.

"Aye, Tom. Weather's set fair. Did you not do so at Lavenham?"

"Why, no," said I, for indeed when a piece was completed and came off the loom it was taken away and we saw no more of it.

"Ah, you've a lot to learn, Tom," said Mr. Firth, shaking his head comfortably. "But never mind; you're a willing lad, I can see that. I daresay you'll do well enough come a month or two. Draw up to the fire, Tom, you must be starved to death out there." By "starved" he meant, as I learned later, "very cold."

"He'd be better to go up to bed and get his sleep," said Mrs. Firth without looking up from her needles. "He can hardly hold his head up as it is."

"Well, happen so," agreed Mr. Firth. "Off with you, lad."

"And where is he to sleep, pray?" said Mrs. Firth acidly. "You have given no thought to that, Stephen."

"Jeremy and I will knock a bed together for him tomorrow."

"What about tonight?"

"If it please you, mistress, there are some old pieces in the workshop where I could very well sleep tonight," I said hastily, not wishing to become an object of contention between man and wife, nor to share a room with Jeremy.

"It's a good notion," said Mr. Firth. "Let it be so, Meg."

"I will get you a coverlet," said Mrs. Firth, rising.

She opened a press and drew out a thick woolen cover.

"Give him a candle, wife," said Mr. Firth.

"He doesn't need a candle," snapped Mrs. Firth. "There's moonlight enough."

So I took the coverlet and bade them good night—to which Mr. Firth replied heartily, Mrs. Firth with her disapproving air—and climbed the stairs in darkness, and I spread the coverlet over the pile of cloth and smoothed it out, in darkness too. Then I cried out and started back, for something had torn a deep scratch on my hand. I sucked the wound and looked more carefully, and there in the moonlight two green orbs gleamed, as Sandy the cat turned his head.

"Well, it's certain nobody wants me here," I said.

Jeremy hated me, little Gracie scowled at me, Mrs. Firth abominated me, Mr. Firth had been persuaded into taking me against his will. Now even the cat resented me. It was the last straw. I had either to laugh or cry. I was ashamed to cry, so I laughed and put out a hand and stroked Sandy's head.

"I mean thee no harm, pussy," said I jokingly. "If this is thy usual couch, bed here with me."

After a moment, enjoying my caress I suppose, the cat began to purr, then he rolled over on his back and played paws with me, keeping his claws now carefully sheathed. The end of it was we lay down together, with Sandy curled into my side, his head on my ribs, my arm round his flanks. I own I took some comfort from his friendliness and the warmth and softness of his fur.

4   A Peddler Calls

I AM WRITING down only those events which really concern the thefts and their discovery, but it is surprising how many things, appearing very small at the time, turned out to matter. The cat Sandy, for instance, had quite an important part to play, though little he knew it, and so had the taking-in doors. However, the next thing of importance that happened was the visit of the peddler.

I was wakened the morning after my arrival at Upper High Royd by the voices of Jeremy and Mr. Firth above my head.

"—a lazy, idle, good-for-nothing, like all these apprentices," Jeremy was concluding in his tone of malice.

"Nay, let the lad sleep. He had a hard day yesterday," said Mr. Firth.

I started up and threw off my coverlet and began to apologize for my late rising, rather confusedly I admit, for I was still half asleep. Mr. Firth sent me down to wash at the trough, and while I was about this Gracie came dancing out and told me to go into the house for something to eat. She was a merry little thing, and I was sorry she still spoke very coldly to me. Mrs. Firth too had not a word for me when I went in, but for all that ladled me out a good portion of oatmeal porridge. I had hardly finished when Mr. Firth shouted to me from above stairs to stay down and help Josiah outside. I went out and saw an elderly grizzled man crossing the yard, carrying a piece of cloth across one shoulder, his arm akimbo on his hip to support its weight. I followed him round the corner of the house; the doors of the taking-in place had been flung back, and Jeremy stood in the opening, letting down a huge hook on the end of a rope which ran over a pulley. Sandy with his paws tucked in lay comfortably to one side, surveying the scene from half-shut eyes, and Mr. Firth leaned out behind him.

"I'm coming down to thee, Josiah," cried Mr. Firth. "Come into th'house and I'll pay thee now. Lap piece up in this, Tom."

He threw down one of the fents of cloth I had slept on. It clanged as it hit the ground, and I saw that metal rings had been fastened to the four corners. I opened this out, and Josiah threw his piece down on it and then went off to the house door. Gracie came dancing to the corner and stood watching as the hook descended slowly to the level of my hands. Where she stood she was out of sight of Jeremy, or he would have behaved differently, no doubt; as it was, thinking himself unobserved he cried: "Dang thee, cat, get out o' my way," and gave Sandy a sharp kick.

Taken at a disadvantage Sandy flew through the air with a piteous mew. Gracie screamed and I put out my arms and caught him. It was more by good luck than by management, I admit, but as I held him against my shoulder and felt his quick heartbeats and saw the look of fright in his great green eyes, I felt glad I had been handy. Gracie ran to me and I put him in her arms.

"You horrid man!" cried Gracie to Jeremy, tilting her head back to look at him. "You kicked my cat."

"Nay, now, Miss Gracie," said Jeremy, a trifle flustered. "I didn't kick him, I just stumbled over him, like."

Gracie looked at me, and I am sure she read in my face that this was a lie.

"Cats always fall on their feet, any road," said Jeremy.

"Now what's all this?" demanded Mr. Firth, coming round

the house at a run. "What are you screaming for, Gracie?"

"Jeremy kicked Sandy out of the taking-in place," said Gracie, "and Tom caught him."

"Now, master, you know I wouldn't kick Miss Gracie's cat," said Jeremy smoothly. "I stumbled over him and the cat fell out on his own."

"The cat shouldn't be up in the workshop in any case," cried Mrs. Firth sharply from the porch.

"I reckon Tom took him up there," said Jeremy.

"Tom caught him," said Gracie. "Jeremy kicked him."

"Now, lovey, now," said Mr. Firth soothingly. "Jeremy didn't mean to harm Sandy."

Gracie gave a little snort. I could not but smile; though Gracie is but a child, I thought, she is shrewder than her father.

"Be off with you to your mother, child," said Mr. Firth.

He pushed her gently toward the porch. But Gracie hung back and looked at me over her shoulder.

"Thank you for catching Sandy, Tom," she cried.

I smiled at her, and felt friendly. But I hid my smile and my thoughts, and bent over the hook, threading it through the rings so that Josiah's piece hung from the hook in a kind of parcel, for Jeremy was my enemy already (heaven knew why) and I did not wish to increase his dislike of me further.

"Go up and help Jeremy haul the piece in," commanded Mr. Firth.

I did so; it came up easily enough as we hauled the rope.

"Does Mr. Firth employ other weavers to weave for him, then?" I asked.

"Only one," said Jeremy with contempt. "He likes to call himself a clothier, but he's not much more than a common weaver to my mind. Now I've worked for a man who was a right clothier, a right manufacturer, as they call them nowadays; he had twenty weavers in his pay."

"I wonder you left him," said I.

My tone was rather sarcastic, for I disliked to hear good Mr. Firth diminished; besides, I thought that a man who had a cow and a horse and a field of oats and a journeyman weaver and an apprentice in his house and one cottage weaver weaving for him was more than a mere weaver. Jeremy gave me one of his evil glances.

"It'll be long before you're a weaver, or anything at all beside a pauper nuisance," he said. "Get on with your carding."

Presently Josiah left and Mr. Firth came up, and there was a long discussion between him and Jeremy, in which I was glad to see Mr. Firth assert his authority. Jeremy wanted to take Josiah's piece down to the fulling mill in the valley—where it would be beaten upon in water by the great wooden stocks, to bring the threads together—that morning, but Mr. Firth said his own piece was nearly finished, and he would take the two pieces down by horseback tomorrow. Jeremy argued this beyond the limits of civility, I thought, but Mr. Firth would not give way, so Jeremy returned to his loom with an ill grace. He was threading the threads of yarn through the healds and the reed with a hook —always a delicate job—when Gracie suddenly bounced into the workshop, her hair a ball of fire in the sunlight.

"A peddler's come and mother says will you please come down to him, Father," she said.

Mr. Firth groaned, but threw his legs over the loom bench and rose, obediently.

"What a woman can spend wi' a peddler is nobody's business," said he ruefully as he left the room.

To my surprise Jeremy threw down his hook and glided after him. I went on carding for a minute or two, but then my curiosity got the better of me and I followed them. Again I was surprised, for at the turn of the stairs I almost crashed into Jeremy, who was crouched down behind the balustrade, watching unseen. I crouched down myself beside him. Jeremy gave me an evil glance but said nothing.

The peddler had come inside the house and taken off his pack, and was standing by the door with his tray in front of him, slung by a leather band about his neck. He was giving one of those quick, glib speeches which all peddlers seemed to abound in, praising his goods to Mr. and Mrs. Firth and Gracie, who all stood in front of him gazing at his tray; Mrs. Firth seemed quite enthralled.

"Ribbons, buttons, hooks and eyes, scissors, gloves, tapes, caps, aprons, all of the very best quality. Ah, madam, now there you have some of the finest silk on the market," he said, as Mrs. Firth fingered a patterned piece of stuff. "I salute your taste. Woven in London—pure silk—came overland from far Cathay. Costly, as is natural—" here Mrs. Firth dropped the silk, "but very fine. Or would little Missie like a ribbon for a knot? Hard-wearing—delightful blue— just the color for Missie's golden hair."

He put out a hand and made to stroke Gracie's head, but she shrank back, for which I was glad, as, for what reason I know not, I did not like this peddler. Yet he was a handsome enough fellow in his way; a pale plump face very clean and closely shaven, a sparkling eye, a good tiewig well curled and tied in a neat black bow, a short round body, a well-shaped leg, and a very fresh-looking suit of bright green cloth with brass buttons. His stockings were scarlet and his shoes had big square buckles. He did not speak with a Yorkshire voice, but to me he seemed too smooth and mincing in his talk, even for one of his trade, who are noted for their eloquence.

"Now those mittens you are holding, madam," he went on, "I might have known you'd pick out those—they are, I assure you, the very best of their kind. Knitted in Dent, in the north of Yorkshire—I'm sure you've heard of Dent, madam, it's noted for its stockings, gloves and mittens. Pure wool throughout. Two colors, as you see. Handsome pattern. Or, if you prefer, madam, I can order you a special pair, with the initial letters of your name knitted in at the wrist. M.F. that would be, would it not?"

At this moment Jeremy sprang up, dragging me with him. We made quite a clatter between us, and drew the peddler's eye. His glance swept over us, cold as a snake's. Mr. Firth looked up, too.

"Well, come down if you wish, don't stand poking about in a corner up there," he said crossly. "If you want to buy owt, Jeremy, get it bought quickly and get back to your work. As for you, Tom, you've no money to buy owt with, so be off with you."

"An apprentice has no need to buy owt, master," put in Jeremy in an agreeing, obsequious tone.

"Well, you can stay for a minute if you like, Tom," said Mr. Firth, whose second thoughts, as I had already discovered, were always kinder than his first, particularly if someone had agreed with him.

I followed Jeremy down the stairs.

"I had the good fortune to see your honored father yester evening, Mistress Firth," said the peddler.

"Indeed?" cried Mrs. Firth in a flutter. "You were at Clough End? You saw my father? How is he?"

"Mr. Sykes is well, madam, and commends himself warmly to you," said the peddler.

Somebody gave a sigh as of relief, but I could not tell from whom it came.

"I am glad to hear that, very glad," said Mr. Firth heartily. "My wife has been anxious, and over there by Almondbury, right beyond Huddersfield, you know, is quite some distance away, so it's not easy for us to get news.

I am obliged to you, peddler, for your message. Come, wife, buy something. What do you fancy, eh?"

"I wouldn't mind a pair of mittens," said Mrs. Firth in a shy, pleased tone.

"Aye, to be sure, have some mittens, love."

"Have some knitted for you with your letters on," urged the peddler. "Then you can choose your own colors. I shall be back with them in a week or two."

"Well—gray, with a brightish blue, then," said Mrs. Firth.

"Gray with a bright blue, from Dent, it shall be."

"Father," said Gracie in a pleading tone, clutching at his hand, "will you buy me something?"

"Of course I will, lovey. What do you fancy?"

Gracie stretched up toward him and he stooped to her and she put her arms round his neck and whispered in his ear.

"Well, well," said he, laughing. "It shall be so. Child wants to buy summat to give to Tom," he said to Mrs. Firth.

The peddler, scenting business, at once stooped down to bring his tray to the level of Gracie's eyes.

"She's not called on to do any such thing, that's certain," cried Mrs. Firth, vexed. "I never heard anything so nonsensical."

"He saved my cat when Jeremy kicked him," said Gracie. She stuck out her underlip and looked ready to cry, and Mrs. Firth yielded.

"Well—choose something sensible, then," she said. "A few buttons, maybe, or a reel of thread."

But Gracie had already seized upon a small pair of scissors.

"These," she said.

"Pure Sheffield steel," said the peddler at once.

Mr. Firth looked a trifle daunted, for doubtless the scissors would be of more price than he wished to pay.

"Why do you choose these, Gracie?" he said reproachfully.

"They're like yours, Father," replied the child.

"She is right there, master," put in Jeremy. "They are real clothier's scissors, with square ends—no points to pierce the cloth."

"Well, take them, child," said Mr. Firth, putting his hand into his pocket for silver. "And you, Tom, see you guard them carefully."

"I will, sir," I said. "Thank you, Miss Gracie."

I spoke strongly, for though I was embarrassed I was indeed touched by the gift. Gracie took the scissors and laid them in my hand, and the touch of her soft little fingers seemed to soothe my sore heart. I could easily have kissed the child as she looked up at me, for she was a sweet little thing, her blue eyes kind and smiling, her hair all red-gold in the sun; but with Mrs. Firth looking down her nose at me with an offended air I did not venture to do so.

"Let it be a sign to you that you'll be a clothier one day, Tom," said Mr. Firth. "Now, then! Let us get back to work."

Upstairs, I put the scissors in the inner pocket of my coat where they fitted as if it had been made for them, and I made up my mind I would keep them there always. The morning passed pleasantly enough, for even Jeremy seemed in a better mood than I had so far seen him.

That night as I lay in my bed I heard a faint mew at my door. At first I disregarded it, but the mew came again, and this time there came a scratching too.

"It is Sandy again," I thought, amused.

I could not help but be pleased though a little concerned, when, as I opened the door, Sandy sprang past me, leaped on my bed and buried himself in the coverlet. I had to move him a little to get myself comfortable, but though he mewed rather pettishly he did not withdraw but adapted himself to my shoulder, and we slept side by side. What Mrs. Firth would have said to this I did not like to think, but I was glad of his company. From that time on he often shared my bed, and indeed his presence was one of the small pleasures of my life.

Indeed, I would have liked my life at Upper High Royd well enough, save for the one matter of Jeremy. Of course I was always hard at work. I helped Josiah to dye the wool in the little round lead house across the yard—a bright blue was the usual Upper High Royd color, and I wore my old ragged clothes on dyeing day. I carried wool out to the women who did carding and spinning for Mr. Firth in their cottages, and I brought the spun yarn back to Upper High Royd for Mr. Firth and Jeremy to weave, or took it out to the cottage of Josiah, and I helped Jeremy when he was warping, and I helped tread the pieces in human water when they were woven, so as to get the grease out of the wool. I hadn't my full strength as yet, so I couldn't carry a piece of cloth down to the fulling mill in the valley or back up the long hills, but I helped to stretch it out on the tenters when it came back dripping water. The pieces from Josiah had to be fulled and tentered too. Then there was the horse to feed and groom, and the cow to milk; and whenever I had nothing else to be busy with I was set to carding. Sometimes Gracie was set to carding too, and when the weather came more summery and warm, we sat side by side in the porch at this task. Sometimes we fell to laughing and talking, and sometimes Mr. Firth would shout down the stairs to us: "Less noise, you two!" But he was never vexed with Gracie for long. It seemed from what I heard from Jeremy that Mr. and Mrs. Firth for long had no children, Mrs. Firth being of a somewhat delicate disposition, and so they cherished Gracie, when she came, particularly.

Meanwhile Mrs. Firth was busy spinning at her wheel; she was indeed a notable spinner, the yarn she spun was very fine and even. Mr. Firth preferred his wife's yarn to any other, so he had Josiah's daughter come to the house to help his wife with domestic tasks, so as to give her more time to spin.

Every Saturday Mr. Firth went to Halifax to market. It was a great business getting him off very early, grooming and saddling the horse, laying the piece of cloth across his saddlebow. Mrs. Firth laid out his market clothes the night before, with his good wig and his newly-starched neckcloth, and I had to polish his riding boots and Bess's harness—

Bess was the name of our sturdy little mare. I could not see why he had to set off so exceedingly early, but it seemed the Cloth Hall, where the cloth was sold, opened punctually at six with the ringing of a bell, and in a few minutes all the cloth for sale was brought in, the merchants entered and the doors closed again, and in an hour or so all the cloth was sold. I wished very much to see this market and the town of Halifax, and one Friday plucked up courage to ask Mr. Firth to let me go next day. I could set off very early on foot, and meet him at the inn where he put up his horse.

"It's a goodish walk, Tom," said he, "and you don't know the way."

"I could easily find it if you gave me directions, master," I said eagerly.

"Aye. And there are signposts," put in Jeremy.

I was surprised by this support from Jeremy, as he usually crossed my wishes if he could, and next time we were alone together I thanked him. He gave me one of his sneering smiles.

"You've a mind to run away and think to slip off in the Halifax crowds, eh, Tom?" he said.

"No!" I replied indignantly. "I am bound apprentice, and shall keep my time. Where could I run to, in any case?"

"Aye, that's true. Where could you run to?" said Jeremy thoughtfully.

My hopes for the morrow were dashed at suppertime, however, by Mrs. Firth, who, when the project was mooted by her husband, asked crossly why I should miss a day's work to no purpose.

"And there's his dinner at the inn, and wear and tear of shoe leather. What are you thinking of, husband?"

"I could take some bread and meat with me," I suggested.

"Disposing of your master's goods now, are you?" began

Mrs. Firth, tossing her head. "At my father's nothing of that sort would have been allowed."

"Enough, Meg!" said Mr. Firth. "Don't put yourself about. I shall not take the lad tomorrow."

I was keenly disappointed, as I had longed for this treat, and I think Mr. Firth was sorry, for next day he very kindly brought back from Halifax a blanket to go on the bed which he and Jeremy had made for me. With summer coming I did not need this extra covering so much, but I should be glad enough of it in the winter. For in these Pennine hills the wind blows often and it is cold.

As to this bed I must say a word because it played its part in the theft story.

As a baby Gracie had slept in a little cot in her parents' bedchamber, but only a year before, Mrs. Firth had put her into a little room of her own, and Gracie was proud of this and did not wish to leave it. Jeremy slept in a large room at the back of the house, where there was space for another bed, and Mr. Firth took it for granted that I should sleep there. But this prospect was hateful to me, and luckily Jeremy disliked it also. He expressed his opposition to sharing a bedchamber with me in terms so opprobrious and insulting that I could have struck him, but since his wish coincided with mine, I held my peace and stood motionless, though I know my face was scarlet with fury. The only sleeping place left open to me was the workshop. Mrs. Firth objected strongly to this at first, but on my promising to open door and window as soon as I rose in the morning, at length agreed.

One very pleasant thing happened to me during these months. One morning there was a knock at the house door, and on my running down to answer it, Mrs. Firth having her hands in pastry at the time, I found Harry Norton standing there. Of course I showed him in, though Mrs.

Firth was a good deal flustered at being caught in her apron, pastry-making. I went up to fetch Mr. Firth from the workshop, but was soon called down again. By this time Mrs. Firth had recovered her composure and was laughing with Harry, who sat in Mr. Firth's chair by the fire, drinking a glass of milk and eating oatcake with a plate of butter beside him.

"Well, Tom," said Mr. Firth cheerfully. "Here is Master Harry Norton come to ask you to spend the day with him on the moors. Wouldst like to go, eh?"

"Yes, sir," I said eagerly. "If you can spare me."

"Why, to oblige Sir Henry I would do a much greater thing," said Mr. Firth. "It seems Sir Henry is away on public business, and Mr. Harry's tutor is away to see a sick relative, and so he is alone."

"I have some provisions," said Harry.

"Go up, Tom, take off your apron, and brush your clothes," said Mr. Firth. "We don't want wool blowing all over Master Harry off you. Wife, put up some meat for Tom. Now, if it should rain, Master Harry, and from the look o' t'sky it well might, don't you hesitate to come back to Upper High Royd. We can give you a bite of dinner, you know."

So we two lads went off together. First we scrambled down a very steep path to one of the valleys, then we climbed up a lane on the far side, up and up, till we passed all the houses and left fields and walls behind, and were right out on the open moorland. Rough grass, somber heather, dark peaty soil, and everywhere little brown becks tumbling downward over rocky beds. The wind blew, the sun shone; larks sang overhead, lapwings (their green backs so dark they looked black, their undersides white) somersaulted in great swift curves overhead; Harry fell to singing and I joined him, and we were happy.

When we stopped to eat our meat in the shelter of a

dip in the moor we were so high that we could see for miles around, a landscape of rising and falling hills dotted here and there with homesteads, with Halifax lying on a slope in the distance. From here the hill on which Barseland stood, high as it was, lay far below us. The air was so clear we could see the Fleece Inn, and the cluster of trees and bushes which hid Sir Henry's mansion, and Upper High Royd, and even the tenters in the tentercroft beside the house, a piece of blue cloth on them bright in the sunshine. I pointed it out to Harry.

"Aye, I see it," he said. "Of all the daft customs, this of leaving cloth out on the tenters all night is the daftest. My father is away to Halifax this morning to confer about it. For the past five weeks there has been cloth stolen in the neighborhood every week. But for heaven's sake," he added hastily, "do not, I pray you, mention it to Mrs. Firth while I am with you. I do not fancy a woman in a screaming fit, and Mrs. Firth is nervous and somewhat given to emotions."

"Yes—but for all that Mrs. Firth is a good and kind woman," said I. "Her bark is worse than her bite, as they say."

"You're content at Upper High Royd, then, are you?"

"I should be well content," I said, "if it were not for Jeremy, who loses no chance to work me ill."

"He looks a sullen sort of chap," said Harry.

"He is always mislaying things and blaming me to Mr. Firth for it, and complaining that I am slow and idle. I am not idle, Harry," I said firmly.

Harry looked at me. "I believe you, Tom," he said.

"Mr. Swain had cloth stolen from his tenters," I reminded him. "Has Sir Henry not discovered who was the thief?"

Harry was silent for so long, I feared I had vexed him.

"I did not mean that as a reproach to Sir Henry," I said.

"Listen, Tom," said Harry. "But mind, do not repeat what I say to you to anyone. Do you remember when we first quarreled?"

"That I do."

"What did we fight about, eh?"

"My father's watch," said I sadly, for as I spoke my former life and Lavenham and my father all came back to me.

"Just so. Now my father bought the watch from a reputable watchmaker in Bradford, who had bought it cheap from a countryman he did not know. The countryman cannot be traced. But it is thought that a man who would steal a watch from a drowning man would not scruple to steal cloth from tenters."

"I never thought of that!" I cried.

"Well, think of it now. But keep your thoughts to yourself. Here comes the rain!" cried Harry suddenly, springing up. "We must get down to shelter."

We were well soaked by the time we reached Upper High Royd. Mrs. Firth made a great fuss over Harry, drying his clothes, and—to be fair—she showed some concern over me, too. She persuaded Harry to stay for his dinner, and gave us a good meal, at which Harry chattered and laughed and kept us all in a good humor—except Jeremy, of course, who sat silent and scowling and rather subdued.

"May Tom come out with me again sometimes, Mr. Firth?" said Harry as he made his farewells.

"Aye, so long as he doesn't leave his work undone," said Mr. Firth rather doubtfully.

"On Sunday afternoons perhaps?" suggested Harry.

Mr. Firth looked at his wife to see what she thought of this. To my surprise she nodded. As Mr. Firth said: "Very well," he seemed rather surprised too.

Mrs. Firth was a little kindlier in manner to me after

that day. Partly because she was pleased to have Sir Henry Norton's son dining in her house and I had brought him there, but partly, I think, for a better reason, namely that Harry set me laughing and chattering with the rest, so that I was more my natural cheerful self than the silent and perhaps morose lad she had previously taken me to be.

But Jeremy's ill-will toward me seemed continually to deepen.

On the very next Saturday after Harry's visit he gave me a real fright. Mr. Firth was off long since to market when Josiah came in with a woven piece. Jeremy sent me down to attach it to the hook as I had done before, and threw the wrapping cloth with the rings down out of the taking-in place with such force that had I been under it (as I nearly was) my neck could well have been broken. Angered and startled, I began to get the wrapping round the piece, thinking to myself that Saturdays, when Mr. Firth was absent, were really very disagreeable days at Upper High Royd. In the porch Mrs. Firth was arguing sharply with Josiah as she paid him.

I knew why she was upset. Getting a piece dried on the tenters in time for Saturday market was always an anxious matter because of the uncertain weather, so the earlier in the week a piece was fulled in the fulling mill down in the valley, the better for the clothier. A custom had therefore grown up among the Barseland clothiers of taking pieces to be fulled on Sunday. This was quite illegal and Sir Henry disapproved of it, but Jeremy was all for it and Mr. Firth was inclined to be led by the other clothiers. Mrs. Firth disliked the custom strongly—nothing like that, of course, had ever been done at her father's—and so it vexed her when Josiah brought a finished piece on Saturday because of the temptation it offered Mr. Firth over this Sunday fulling. So she snapped at Josiah in her shrill voice till (luckily for me)

Gracie tired of it and ran into the yard to be out of the way.

For just as I grasped the big hook in one hand to put it through the rings, there was a sudden violent jerk and I found myself swinging in mid-air. Jeremy had hauled on the rope. I brought my other hand to the hook quickly, and held on; I had no desire to fall ten feet, especially with those iron rings below me.

"Jeremy! Let me down!" I cried.

I had thought, of course, that this was just a spiteful joke, very uncomfortable for me but not meant to be dangerous, but as I looked up into Jeremy's face I felt a pang of fear; such a look of hatred, of evil will, I had never seen in any man's eyes before. Moreover, he now wound the end of the rope round its staples in the workshop wall, so that I was held in mid-air; and then, reaching out, he began to sway the rope from side to side, and twist it, so that I spun round. I felt sick and dizzy, and tried to make up my mind to jump, while Jeremy's sneering face seemed to swing back and forward above me, when Gracie screamed suddenly:

"Mother! Mother! Come quick! Mother!"

A scream from Gracie always brought everyone at Upper High Royd to her at the run. So now Mrs. Firth came rushing round the corner, Josiah lumbered after, and Harriet (Josiah's daughter) followed gaping with a broom in her hand.

"What are you about, Jeremy? Let the boy down at once! Josiah, hold him up! Help him down!" shrilled Mrs. Firth, while Josiah shouted:

"Jump, lad! I'll catch thee!"

Gracie broke into loud sobs. Harriet said: "Eh! I never!" and they all stood gazing up at me, their open mouths and upturned eyes giving a comical effect.

Jeremy writhed his face into an expression of surprised consternation, loosed the rope and let me down with a bump.

I fell into Josiah's arms and knocked him over, and we rolled together in the yard.

I own I felt shaken, and did not resist when Mrs. Firth, calling me "Poor lad," led me into the house and put me into a chair by the fire and brought me a mug of dandelion beer to drink. Jeremy came down and laid his hand as if fondly on my shoulder, with many expressions of regret and explanations how he had not seen me on the hook, he thought it was the piece he was hauling up, and so on. But these were all lies and I shrank from him.

He was very solicitous about me for the next few days, the more so as Mr. Firth, who had doubtless heard all about the hook affair from Mrs. Firth and Gracie, was decidedly ill-tempered with him. To distract Mr. Firth's attention from the matter, as I thought, Jeremy began to be urgent with him to weave broadcloths instead of kerseys. A kersey is usually about a yard (thirty-six inches) wide, whereas a broadcloth is fifty-four inches at least, often more. Broadcloths, of course, command a bigger price than kerseys, not only because they have more stuff in them but because it is easier to cut suits and coats from broader cloth—tailoring from narrow cloth is very wasteful and needs more seams. A broadcloth must be very evenly and closely woven, lest it sag, but as Jeremy kept saying, with Mrs. Firth's fine, even yarn and the good, close weaving of himself and Mr. Firth, he was sure that Upper High Royd broadcloth could soon become quite renowned.

Mrs. Firth could not but be flattered by all this, and pleased, because at her father's they wove broadcloths; and Mr. Firth seemed to be coming gradually round to the idea.

"After all, why keep an apprentice and make no use of him?" urged Jeremy.

"True. Dost think tha could do it, Tom?" said Mr. Firth,

who was apt to become more Yorkshire in his speech when he was out of his wife's hearing.

"He has done it for his father many a time, isn't that so, Tom?" said Jeremy smoothly.

"Why, yes," said I.

The point of this lies in the different widths of the two cloths. With a narrow kersey, the weaver sitting before the loom can slide the shuttle, which is pointed at both ends, through the threads with his right hand, and then slide it back the other way with his left hand. But a broadcloth is too wide for one man to reach both sides, so an apprentice sits at one side of the loom and throws the shuttle at that side, to help the weaver.

"We'll try it. Set a broadcloth up soon's this kersey's finished, Jeremy," said Mr. Firth.

It was promotion for me to be allowed to have anything to do with the weaving, and in a way I felt glad, but somehow the pleased gleam in Jeremy's eyes made me uneasy.

It was in the night before the broadcloth was to be begun —Jeremy had done the warping and looming-up very neatly and skillfully, that day—when I suddenly started awake with a pang of terror. It seemed to me that all of a sudden I saw the true reason for Jeremy's insistence on the broadcloth. I told myself my thought was a coward's thought and I should feel shame for it, but I could not get it out of my head. I could hear voices from the housebody below, so Mr. and Mrs. Firth were still downstairs, and after some tossing and turning I suddenly took my resolution and rose up and drew on my shirt and breeches and went downstairs.

Mrs. Firth was rolling up her knitting, Mr. Firth stood in the open doorway, looking out at the night, which was moonlit and very fine.

"Why, Tom!" said he. "What's up, lad?"

"Mr. Firth," I said in a rush. "I am afraid to weave at the broadcloth with Jeremy."

"Afraid? Nay, Tom!"

"I knew a lad in Lavenham, an apprentice, that was blinded by a shuttle, weaving so; he was not quite quick enough, he did not catch the shuttle, it flew into his eyes. Mr. Firth, Jeremy does not like me. I am ashamed to say it, but I am afraid."

"Well," said Mr. Firth. His face hardened; he stood very still. Mrs. Firth had come up behind us and was leaning against the doorjamb. They exchanged a glance. "Tha did right to speak to me, Tom," said Mr. Firth. "Tha's no need to fear."

Next morning, when Jeremy had put a spindle of yarn into a shuttle and was just "kissing the shuttle," as weavers say, to draw the thread through the hole, ready to begin weaving the broadcloth, Mr. Firth came into the workshop.

"Now, Jeremy," he said. "Just beginning broadcloth, eh?"

"That's right," said Jeremy smugly.

"Sithee, Jeremy," said Mr. Firth—this is a Yorkshire expression meaning *see thee,* that is, *look*. "Sithee, if any harm comes to this lad Tom through t'broadcloth, or in any other way, i' my house, I shall hold thee guilty."

Jeremy started and his sallow face flushed.

"That's not fair, master!" he cried.

"Happen not," said Mr. Firth. "But I mean it, Jeremy. I'll take thee to th'assizes if any harm happens Tom. So think on and watch out."

I came to no harm over the broadcloth.

5 Mr. Daniel Defoe

IT WAS NOW SUMMER. The heather on the moors came into bloom, so that when I went out one Sunday afternoon with Harry, as had become our habit, I was amazed by the great stretches of purple which rolled away on every hand. The cotton grass was out too, clustering in the moorland hollows, the white silky heads dancing in the wind on their slender stems; the green bracken on the middle slopes was almost head-high.

For there was plenty of wind and rain; it was a poor, cold summer. This vexed Mr. Firth, for the season had so far been good and the oats and hay were both well advanced and ready for harvest. However, he and Josiah at length mowed the hay and carried it into the barn, with Mrs. Firth and me and even little Gracie helping to turn and fork it. Jeremy would not lift a hand to help; he said he was a journeyman weaver and had naught ("nowt," as he said) to do with crops. Mr. Firth was put out by this at first, but was glad enough that there was a piece ready for him to take to market on Saturday. He got a good price for it too, for it seemed all clothiers were busy harvesting so there was a scarcity of cloth for sale. Presently he and Josiah harvested the oats together; what with helping in these works and spreading lime on the fields, for some three weeks I was out of doors all day, and what was even better, away from Jeremy; so I grew quite tanned and cheerful.

Then we began to thresh the oats on the threshing floor

beside the barn, and it was here that the accident happened which made me so wretched.

It was a cold, gusty morning, and, though still August, the summit of the highest hills around had a thin covering of snow. Mr. Firth and Josiah and myself were all threshing, that is, banging a flail down on the oats to separate the grain from the husk, so that the wind could blow the light husks away. It is warm work, and in spite of the cold wind I had left my jacket in the house and rolled up my shirt sleeves. Josiah and Mr. Firth were exchanging reminiscences about harvests when Mr. Firth was a boy—Josiah, it seemed, had been apprenticed in those long-ago times to Mr. Firth's father. I was swinging the flail with a will when suddenly with a sharp crack something hit the tip of my elbow. I gave a yelp of pain, for of all places in the body the tip of the elbow is the most sensitive to a blow; my arm went numb, and the flail flew out of my hand. I was bent over double, rubbing my arm and exclaiming at the pain, when I heard a roar from Mr. Firth, who was hopping about and then clinging to the side of the barn, his face distorted with pain and rage; my flail had flown through the air and come down heavily on his foot. Josiah and I both ran to him and held him up, for he could not put his foot to the ground.

"I am sorry, master," I cried. "Something hit my elbow."

"Dang thee for a daft clumsy blockhead!" he shouted. "Wherever tha goes, summat goes wrong!"

He struck at me with the back of his fist, and the blow fell on my cheek.

"You'd best carry me to the house," he said. "I can do no more here."

Josiah and I crossed hands beneath him and he put his arms round our shoulders, and so we carried him, roaring and swearing. In the yard we met Jeremy, whose look of

consternation gave me a grim pleasure; he had not meant to hurt Mr. Firth, I judged, when he threw the stone at me.

We seated Mr. Firth in his armchair by the fire and Mrs. Firth ran to him and pulled off his shoe and stocking; she felt his foot with some skill, and said she thought that though it was severely bruised, no bones were broken. But Mr. Firth did not believe her.

"Josiah, be off down the valley and fetch me the surgeon," he said.

"Shall I go, master?" I suggested timidly.

"No! You'd get lost or bring me the blacksmith," snorted Mr. Firth. "Ill luck attends owt you do."

Josiah set off, and I went back to the threshing floor.

I own I felt very wretched and also resentful. There on the ground lay the stone which had made me loose the flail; a nasty sharp-pointed piece of millstone grit, as they call the very hard stone round here. That Jeremy had thrown it I did not doubt. I was grieved and troubled over Mr. Firth's foot. But although I knew his quick fiery temper, and knew too that his first angry responses were often softened by his second more kindly thoughts, I could not help resenting his blow. It was not so much the pain of it, though my cheek stung; it was the indignity. There is something about a blow which insults a man. A boy feels insult as much as a man, I thought; more perhaps. It is wrong for a man to strike an apprentice, who has not the right to strike back. Besides, it was not true that things went wrong wherever I was; what had gone wrong since I came to Upper High Royd? All those tales of Jeremy's of me mislaying tools and so on, came to my mind, and it struck me for the first time that Mr. Firth had believed them. But even so, a blow! So I went on, turning the thing over and over in my mind, my resentment continually growing.

Presently the surgeon, as I supposed, came riding up the

lane, clutching his hat in a sudden gusty shower of hail; shortly after he left again, and then Gracie came running out to me, with some bread and cheese for me in her hand.

"Father's foot is not broken, only badly bruised and swollen," she said.

"I am very glad of it," I said in a sulky tone.

"But stay out of his sight, Tom, till he has recovered his temper and forgotten your carelessness," she said.

"It was not my carelessness," I said angrily. "A stone hit my elbow and numbed my arm. Here is the stone. Who threw it you may guess if you wish."

Gracie said nothing, but stood weighing the stone in her hand thoughtfully. Then all of a sudden she ran off toward the house, carrying the stone with her.

I had finished my bread and cheese and was hard at work again—for I determined not to be accused of neglecting my duty—when I heard a sound of jingling bits and horses' hoofs, and then the barking of a small dog. I looked up, and saw a company of five coming up the lane on horseback, two of them by their dress servants, the leader holding within the breast of his coat a small young spaniel dog, which was yapping at Sandy, who lay along the top of the tentercroft wall in the sheltered corner, with his paws tucked in, half asleep. I was astonished by so much company in this remote place, the more so as none of them had faces which I knew. Sandy awoke and looked at them wearily, ready to be off if the dog struggled free, but his master held him firmly and ruffling his head bade him be quiet.

"Now, my boy," said this man in a friendly tone to me: "Tell me, if you please, are we in the right way for Halifax?"

"You are hardly in the right way for anywhere up here, sir," said I. "Halifax lies over there." I pointed.

"Kindly direct me to the right way, then," said he.

He spoke so pleasantly, with such easy assurance and cheerful friendliness, that I quite took a fancy to him. Though rather slight and spare in build, with a brown complexion and a large mole at the left side of his mouth, he somehow dominated his companions; and this was because of some quality in himself rather than owing to his full-bottomed wig and his good dark gray suit, though this went well with his keen gray eyes.

"I would not presume to do so, sir," I said, hesitating. "But if you would come into the house, Mr. Firth could tell you."

"What! Live within sight of a town and not know the way to it?" said one of the other men, laughing.

"The boy is a stranger to the place; can't you hear he does not speak with a north-country voice?"

"Aye, you're right, Mr. Defoe," said the man who had laughed at me. "As usual. Take us to your master, lad."

"Where do you come from? Lavenham! I have been in Suffolk. How long have you been in Yorkshire? Why did you come? Are you an apprentice? How long are you bound for? What trade are you learning?"

These and other questions were fired at me by this Mr. Defoe as we passed between the barn and the yard, so that from my stammered answers he had my whole story out of me before we reached the house. I went in and said—for I was still sore about the blow:

"Some gentlemen wish to ask for directions to Halifax."

Mr. Firth was sitting with his foot, all bandaged, up on a stool; Mrs. Firth was spinning, Gracie was carding, I could hear the sound of the shuttle flying in the loom, upstairs. There was a blazing coal fire, as usual; but I was somewhat taken aback to see the stone which had struck my elbow lying in the center of the table.

I marveled much to see how Mr. Defoe set us all at ease.

"Your servant, sir. Pray pardon this intrusion. Madam, your servant." He bowed very politely to Mrs. Firth, who looked pleased and flustered. "We are traveling from Rochdale to Halifax, and have lost our way in these hills of yours. These gentlemen are Rochdale merchants. My name is Daniel Defoe, merchant, of London."

"London!" said Mr. Firth. "You are a long way from home, sir. Pray be seated. Wife, some ale."

"You do not know my name?" said Mr. Defoe, laughing pleasantly.

"Why, no—I regret," stumbled Mr. Firth.

"*Robinson Crusoe* has not yet reached Yorkshire, then. That is hard, seeing I wrote much of it in Halifax," said Mr. Defoe. "Well! Yorkshire has that pleasure to come."

"My father has a copy of the book," said Mrs. Firth in her genteelest tone—she was delighted to welcome a man from the great world of London.

"Pray give him my compliments, Madam, and my hopes that he enjoyed the book. I wrote it," said Mr. Defoe, laughing pleasantly again, "and I am glad it has been well received. But enough of my affairs. May I inquire what is the sound I hear, above?"

"It's the loom—the shuttle in the loom. My journeyman weaver is busy weaving cloth."

"Ah. Cotton cloth?"

"No, no!" said Mr. Firth indignantly. "All wool."

"Are you, then—"

"A clothier? Yes. We've always been clothiers in this house."

Mr. Defoe went off again into a whirl of questions: how long had Mr. Firth lived at Upper High Royd? His father? His grandfather too? Farmers too? No? Partly farmers, always clothiers? Was it not inconvenient, living so far from a town? What day was Halifax market? How many pieces of cloth did Mr. Firth weave a week? A journeyman weaver too? Where did the coals come from?

"Tom, help your mistress to pour the ale," said Mr. Firth, rather flustered by all these questions.

"Why, boy, what a bruise you have there!" said Mr. Defoe, seizing me by the arm and turning up my elbow for all to see. "How did you come by that, eh?"

"A stone struck me," I muttered, hanging my head.

"That is the stone," piped up Gracie, pointing to the stone lying on the table.

"A sharp little maid, as well as a pretty one," said Mr. Defoe, smiling at Gracie—the spaniel puppy had laid its head on her knee and was gazing up at her in that yearning way spaniels have.

"Tom, pour yourself a mug of ale," said Mr. Firth gruffly.

I could see he now thought he had misjudged me about the falling flail, and this was a great relief to me. It struck me, too, that since the loom was still plying upstairs—Jeremy being usually eager to come down to see any visitors—there had perhaps been sharp words between Jeremy and Mr. Firth about the stone. I felt as if a weight had rolled off my shoulders.

"Do you make kerseys here, or broadcloths? Do you dye and finish them yourself? I see the little maid is busy. I should be greatly obliged, Mr. Firth, if you would give me a comprehensive account of the cloth industry of the West Riding."

Mr. Firth, who was clearly still shaken and in pain from the accident to his foot, appeared somewhat daunted by this demand, and hesitated.

"My inquiries are not made from personal curiosity, I assure you, sir," said Mr. Defoe. "I am preparing a book to be called *A Tour of England and Wales,* and naturally I wish to give a clear and full account of all the places I visit. I am ignorant of this cloth trade of yours. I wish to perceive the reason and nature of the thing."

Mr. Firth, poor man, quite gasped, while Mrs. Firth and Gracie urged him:

"Come along, Stephen."

"To be in a book, Father!"

Mr. Defoe perceived Mr. Firth's distress. (What did he not perceive? It seemed to me his shrewd eyes saw everything.) With a true friendliness, which I admired, he relieved his host's embarrassment by going on easily: "But you are so familiar with the trade, it is difficult for you to take an outside view of it. Now, Tom here, who knows it so much less, may see it so much the more clearly. Come, Tom, begin. Why is almost every man in these hills a clothier?"

"The land is harsh and not good to grow crops, but the grass and heather and bracken will feed sheep, so there is wool."

"But do not the clothiers buy wool from southern counties? I have heard so."

"The wool is longer and finer in Suffolk and those southern parts," explained Mr. Firth, "but in early times, when weaving began here, it was because we had the wool."

"And the water, master," said I.

"Aye! That's right. We need water, you see, to wash the wool and the cloth and full the cloth, and we've plenty of becks running down the hillsides. And rivers in the valleys to turn the water wheels of the fulling mills."

"Good. I understand that. Now, Tom, tell me how the cloth is made."

"Well, every Saturday Mr. Firth rides to market—"

"I shan't be able to get my foot into the stirrup this Saturday, I'll be bound."

"—and he brings home a pack of wool. And then Jeremy and I—"

"Jeremy's the journeyman weaver?"

"Yes. We clean the wool of dirt and burrs and twigs, and wash it, and Josiah and I dye it in the lead vat across the yard and leave it out to dry, and then we put it in layers on the floor, and put butter on it—"

"Butter?" exclaimed Mr. Defoe in astonishment.

"Well, grease of any kind. We use butter," said Mr. Firth. "Because we make our own butter, you see."

"And we mix it all up, toss it about. And then Miss Gracie and I, and Josiah's children, we card it. Show Mr. Defoe, Miss Gracie."

"Is it not hard work for the little maid?" said Mr. Defoe, bending to watch her hands.

"Oh, any child over four can do it," said Mr. Firth.

"And then Mrs. Firth and other—wives of the neighborhood," I said, not knowing quite what to call them, "spin the cardings into yarn. We take the wool to their cottages, sometimes quite far afield."

"Ah," said Mr. Firth, shaking his head, "to get a sufficient supply of yarn—that, Mr. Defoe, is always a clothier's difficulty."

"Then Jeremy and Mr. Firth weave the yarn into cloth," I continued, "and then—"

"Hold hard a minute there, Tom," said Mr. Defoe. "Explain to me, please, how weaving is done. Simply and clearly."

"Why, that is very difficult, Mr. Defoe," said I. "For a loom is a very complicated affair."

"Go on, Tom. Just tell me the nature of the process."

"Well, the idea of weaving is to interlace threads of yarn to make a web. First you lay a lot of threads side by side all going in one direction and fastened round a beam at each end. This is the warp. Alternate threads go through healds —like the eyes of needles—which are fastened to a short beam over the loom, and the other threads are fastened in the same way to another beam. These beams are worked by separate treadles. So when you press one treadle down with your foot, one beam rises and one set of threads rises. Then you have a shuttle with a pirn of yarn inside it, and the yarn comes out through a hole. This is the woof. You hold this thread of woof at one side of the loom and press the treadle and slide the shuttle across the loom, and so you see the shuttle takes the thread of woof under one set of warp threads and over the other set. Then you take your foot off that treadle and you press the other treadle and throw the shuttle back, and it takes the woof over the warp threads that were under last time, and under those that were over. And so you make a web. It is like mending a stocking. Of course you have to push the threads against each other between each throw of the shuttle," I added.

"That is quite right, Tom," said Mr. Firth approvingly, "quite right, lad. He's a sharp lad, is Tom, Mr. Defoe. He can read and write both. Except you have left out the reed, Tom, and not mentioned the shed and the—"

"Nay! No more, I beg of you," said Mr. Defoe in haste, smiling, however, to take the sting from his words. "It is above my poor head already. The piece is woven, then. What next?"

"We steep it in human water, like," said Mr. Firth, passing quickly over this disagreeable part of the business, "and then take it down to the fulling mill in the valley, where it is scoured—washed, you would call it—and then fulled, brought together by being beaten by the stocks, like. Then we bring it back home and stretch it on the tenters to dry, and when it's dry I take it to market."

"And what happens in the market?"

"Oh, you'll have to see that for yourself, Mr. Defoe," said Mr. Firth, who was clearly tired of the subject. "There's a market in Halifax on Saturday; you must stay and see it. Now, will you have a bite to eat with us? We're having a leg of mutton, isn't that so, wife?"

"No, no, we mustn't trespass further on your hospitality, Mr. Firth, we've wasted far too much of your time already. I am infinitely obliged to you for your information. Now we must be on our way. As for you, Tom," said Mr. Defoe, rising and smiling, "come out with me and let us see if we can find something for you for your trouble."

"I'll call Jeremy down and he'll set you on your right road," said Mr. Firth. "Or, wait—is Josiah back yet, Tom?"

I ran to the door; Josiah was back at the threshing floor and I called him.

There was a bustle as Mr. Defoe opened one of his saddlebags, the other travelers mounted their horses, Josiah hurried across the yard, the spaniel barked and chased Sandy, who fled into the barn, and Mrs. Firth came into the porch and began saying polite farewells. Mr. Defoe drew out of his saddlebag two small calf-bound volumes and handed them to me.

"Here you are, Tom," said he. "This is *Robinson Crusoe*. You can read, I am told, so I hope you enjoy the tale."

I was so overjoyed that I did not know what to say, but stammered and colored.

"May I keep the volumes, mistress?" I managed at length.

"Of course, Tom," said Mrs. Firth graciously.

"Thank you a thousand times, Mr. Defoe," said I.

It was not only for the gift of the books that I felt thankful to him; his friendly pleasant speech and the interest of his visit had cheered me greatly. But I did not know how to say this, and stood there foolishly, silent.

"Madam," said Mr. Defoe, bowing politely over his saddlebow to Mrs. Firth. "Your most obliged servant."

"Your servant, sir," simpered Mrs. Firth, curtseying very elegantly.

"Follow me," cried Josiah, enjoying the importance of his errand.

He led them off down the lane and suddenly they were gone and all was quiet.

I went soberly upstairs to the workshop.

"What was all that to-do downstairs?" snapped Jeremy, who was looking very pale.

"Travelers asking the way to Halifax," I said.

"Travelers from where?"

"Rochdale and London."

Jeremy threw out a word of contempt for all such travelers, but appeared satisfied.

That evening when work was over and supper cleared, I took out my books, Mr. Defoe's gift, and turned their pages reverently. Their small size, so neat and handy, was a great pleasure to me. The evening was cold and showery, and a great fire as usual blazed on the hearth. Mr. Firth smoked his pipe, Gracie on his knee; Mrs. Firth knitted; Jeremy was out.

"That man is always out," complained Mrs. Firth.

"A man must have a drink at the inn sometimes, Meg," said her husband.

"Why?" snapped Mrs. Firth. "He would be much better without it."

"Is that the book Mr. Defoe gave you, Tom?" asked Mr. Firth, changing the subject.

"I liked Mr. Defoe. He was truly genteel," said Mrs. Firth.

"But no nonsense about him," said her husband. "No nonsense at all. Well, Tom! Lost your tongue?"

"No, master. The book is so—exciting," I said.

"Read us a bit of it, then," said Mr. Firth.

There was a slip of paper between the leaves, about fifty pages on in the first volume, and I had idly begun to read the book there, meaning to go back presently to the beginning. But the tale held me so, I could not leave it.

"It is a shipwreck, and the man who tells it has taken to a boat with the mate and some of the crew," I explained. "Oh heavens! *A raging wave, mountain-like, came rolling astern of us and overset the boat!"*

"Well, go on, go on," said Mr. Firth impatiently.

"Does he get drowned?" cried Gracie, lifting her head from her father's shoulder.

"How could he tell the tale if he got drowned? Go on, Tom."

And so, for an hour that evening and for many evenings later, I read aloud the adventures of Robinson Crusoe; how he was wrecked, how he alone came safe to land on an island, how he had only a knife and a small screw of tobacco on his person, how when the sea calmed he swam out to the wreck and made himself a raft from her timbers and brought back bread and cheese and tools, and how he built a hut for himself with tables and chairs, and how he tamed a parrot and taught it to speak, and how presently he saw the print of a man's foot in the sand! Gracie was so distressed by this that she could hardly sleep that night, and Mrs. Firth was upset by the savage cannibals who visited the island shortly after, but Mr. Firth held fast to his belief that Crusoe could not be telling the tale unless he were still alive, and though in a way this was a confusion, for Crusoe was not real but only a man in a story, in a way he was right. And presently Man Friday came, and we all rejoiced that Crusoe at last had company.

But my interest in Robinson Crusoe is taking me too far ahead; I must go back to the time when I first began to read about this wonderful creation of Mr. Daniel Defoe.

6   At the Market

THE NEXT MORNING after this first reading, word having got round Barseland of Mr. Firth's accident, Mr. Gledhill came up to see him. Gracie came to call me down, for Mr. Gledhill had not seen me since I came to Upper High Royd, except in church at a distance.

"You're to come and be looked at, Tom," said Gracie, laughing.

So I went downstairs feeling uncomfortable. Mr. Firth sat with his foot up, as before.

"My word, he's grown!" said Mr. Gledhill.

"Aye, he's grown a tidy bit since he came, has Tom," said Mr. Firth with satisfaction. "My wife feeds him well, you see."

"And does he frame well, then?" inquired Mr. Gledhill.

This is a Yorkshire expression meaning *show good promise,* so I felt more uncomfortable even than before.

"Not too bad, not too bad," said Mr. Firth, laughing. "Aye, you may say he frames well enough on the whole, does our Tom. Heark'ee, Tom," he went on in a more serious tone, "wouldst like to go to Halifax market on Saturday with Mr. Gledhill, eh?"

"I would indeed," I said eagerly.

"Wilt take the lad, then, Gledhill?"

"Aye—he can ride on the side of the wagon, as I said, if your Jeremy will drive the wagon for me. Our pieces can travel on the wagon together, and I'll ride in as usual on horseback. But I can't sell your piece for you, Firth."

"No, no—Jeremy will do that if you'll vouch him in. I'd send Jeremy in with the piece on horseback, like I take it myself, only Jeremy's no horseman. Nor old Josiah. I don't want Bess's knees broken because she's been let stumble or summat like that." He added, brightening: "My foot may be well enough for me to ride to Halifax on Saturday myself."

"It won't," said Mr. Gledhill laconically.

"Now, Gledhill!"

"You'll not get that foot into a stirrup for a two–three days yet, mark my words."

"And mark mine too," said Mrs. Firth, bustling in.

"Well, thankee, Gledhill, for your offer to take my piece in. I'm much obliged."

"Let them and the piece be down with me early on Saturday, that's all I ask," said Mr. Gledhill, rising to leave.

"I reckon I'll send Josiah down on Friday night with the piece," said Mr. Firth.

"Aye, that'll be best."

On Friday evening Mr. Firth called me to him, and to my astonishment put a fourpenny piece in my hand.

"There's for thy dinner in Halifax tomorrow, Tom." He looked round to see that nobody was near, and went on: "I did wrong to strike thee, but the pain in my foot was sharp. Try to forget it, lad."

"Thank you kindly, Mr. Firth," I said, less for the fourpence than for his regret for the blow.

Jeremy, as I had expected, received the news that I was to accompany him with a very ill grace. After a few expressions of irritation, as that I should be a clog round his neck, that he was not a wetnurse, and so on, he scorned my eagerness to go to Halifax.

"Why are you so eager, eh?" he said. "You think to slip off, do you? You mean to break your apprenticeship and run away?"

"I have told you before, Jeremy," I said angrily, "I am bound to Mr. Firth for seven years and shall keep my indentures."

However vexed he was at the thought of my company there was nothing Jeremy could do against Mr. Firth's orders. So by four o'clock on Saturday morning he and I were sitting on the side of Mr. Gledhill's wagon, with four pieces of cloth behind us, Mr. Gledhill's three maroon and our one blue. Jeremy drove, which he did poorly, I thought; he seemed tired and depressed this morning. For my part I was in great spirits. We set off in the dark, but soon the sun came up and shone brightly, for the weather had taken up and we could see the hills rolling around us for many miles away.

We came down a very steep hillside lane, which I was glad to get to the bottom of, not trusting Jeremy overmuch with the reins, and crossed a ford, which I enjoyed; it was agreeable to see the water splashing round our wheels. Then up another steep hillside and so into the main road to Halifax. This was quite busy with folk going to market; clothiers on horseback with a piece across their saddle, less well-to-do men carrying a piece across their shoulder, their arm akimbo to take the strain; housewives with butter and eggs in baskets; two big wagons each drawn by two horses, piled with cloth. What with the rolling of the wagon wheels, the clop-clop of horses' hoofs, and the chatter of the passing folk, there was quite a hubbub, and this grew louder as we neared the town. Then, too, everyone was wearing their good go-to-market clothes, so there was color everywhere. I thought once I saw the scarlet stockings of the peddler in the distance, but Jeremy turned sharply to the left just then, so I did not get a clear view; besides our peddler was not the only man to wear red stockings.

Presently we passed a very strange kind of wooden frame,

standing on a platform of earth by the side of the road. This platform was walled round, with steps leading up to it, quite solid. I could not make out what the use of the thing could be: there were two tall upright pieces of timber, grooved, and joined near the top by a beam across; within these was a square block of wood, which looked as if it would slide up and down in the groove.

"What is that, Jeremy?" I asked.

"That's the gibbet," he said. "Haven't you heard of Halifax Gibbet Law? Anyone caught stealing cloth from tenters had his head chopped off. The chap was thrown down on the ground, and there was an axe, you see, nailed to that block"—he pointed—"and the block was held up by a rope wound round a peg, and they drew the peg out, and down fell the axe. Whoosh!"

"That's horrible!" I cried.

"Well, you needn't fret yourself, lad; it hasn't been used for seventy years or more," said Jeremy. "Can't you see the axe and the rope aren't there now?"

"I'm glad of that. I suppose the law was so strict because it's so easy to steal cloth from the tenters," I said.

"I daresay. Oh be hanged to the gibbet!" he cried suddenly, touching up the horse with his whip so that it started forward. "It makes one sick to look at the thing."

Indeed he had gone quite pale.

"I agree with you, Jeremy," said I warmly, and for the first time I felt drawn to the man.

A moment later we passed an inn, the sign of which declared it to be the Rose and Crown, and in the doorway who should be standing but Mr. Defoe.

"There's Mr. Defoe!" I cried, waving my hand to him. "Oh, Jeremy, may I go and talk with him? Just for a few minutes?"

"You can do owt you like for owt I care," said Jeremy

roughly. "I don't want to see you again till six o'clock to-night. You can meet me then in the Old Cock yard."

"Very well," said I, delighted.

Mr. Defoe had pushed his way through the crowd and now came up to the wagon, which was halted for me to dismount.

"Well, Tom! Good morning," said he.

"Oh, Mr. Defoe, I am so glad to see you, to tell you how much I am enjoying—we are all enjoying—" I began. Then I remembered my manners, and said: "This is Jeremy Oldfield, journeyman weaver to Mr. Firth. I don't think you saw him at Upper High Royd, he was busy at the loom."

"Morning. No, I didn't see you at Upper High Royd," said Mr. Defoe to Jeremy, who muttered: "Servant," and touched his forelock. "But I saw you last night, I think. In a corner at the inn here. You were arguing some point over a drink of ale with a fellow in scarlet stockings and a man pitted by smallpox."

"Me, sir? No, sir! I wasn't in Halifax last night," cried Jeremy quickly. "You've mistaken your man, sir. You have indeed."

"Well, maybe so," said Mr. Defoe carelessly. "The corner was dark. It's of no consequence."

"We must be off, Tom," said Jeremy, whipping up the horse.

"You said I could talk to Mr. Defoe, Jeremy," I cried, as the wagon wheel nearly knocked me down.

"Do as you like, it's nowt to me if I never see you again," Jeremy threw back over his shoulder.

"A surly, bad-tempered fellow," said Mr. Defoe. "I wonder how your Mr. Firth, who is a cheerful, open kind of man, can bear to keep him."

"He is a good weaver."

"All the same I saw him here last night, talking to scarlet stockings and pockface. Money passed between them."

"Jeremy's time after six is his own. *Robinson Crusoe* is grand, Mr. Defoe!" I burst out, tired of talk about Jeremy.

Mr. Defoe laughed, and jingled the coins in his pocket.

"It must be long hours since you left Upper High Royd, Tom," said he. "Art hungry, lad? Come in and break your fast."

So I very thankfully ate a large plate of fried ham and eggs, often having to answer Mr. Defoe's questions most unbecomingly with my mouth full, for it seemed he was in haste, having arranged to be allowed to enter the Cloth Hall and watch the market there, and so was listening for the bell. Presently it rang and we hurried off together, for I was loath to part with him.

The Cloth Hall seemed to me a poor ordinary place compared with our fine old Guildhall in Lavenham, but as we stood by the broad doors I was certainly astonished by the number of pieces brought in, which I reckoned to be upward of three hundred. Each man brought a piece on his shoulder, but there was no jostling and pushing; they all stood in line and went in smoothly, with scarcely a "by your leave" here and there. Mr. Defoe watched it all with shining eyes, turning his head from side to side and letting nothing escape him. Presently a very well-dressed clothier came up to us.

"Now's your time, Mr. Defoe. Go in quietly and stand by the doors. Don't speak and don't walk about. You'll have to stay in till the bell rings again, you understand?"

"Yes. My boy can come in too, I suppose?" said Mr. Defoe in a careless tone.

"Aye, if he behaves himself. But stand still and don't say a word, lad, or you'll be in trouble."

We had just stepped inside when the bell stopped ringing

and the doors were closed behind us. A group of men who had been standing by the doors at once moved forward away from us, so that now we could see the rows of boards laid on trestles, stretching along each side of the hall. The pieces of cloth were laid across these trestle tables, with a man behind; red and blue and brown and green, they made a pretty sight.

And now the merchants—for such, I now saw, were the group who had been standing by the door—went along to the trestles and began to bargain for the cloth. At least, I suppose they were bargaining, for some of them had patterns of cloth in their hands, which they tried to match up amongst the pieces, and some held papers or letters to which they referred, as if these were their instructions on what to buy. But I could not at first be sure what they were about, for nobody spoke a word aloud. It was all done in whispers. This astonished me, for indeed it had rather a ludicrous effect, these sturdy solid men bending forward to whisper in each other's ears. However, as I grew accustomed to the sight I began, as Mr. Defoe would say, to perceive the reason and nature of the thing. The merchant examined the piece, if he did not like it he moved on; if it suited him he bent forward and asked the price, the clothier whispered it, and the bargain was struck; money changed hands, and the clothier threw the piece over his shoulder and took it out by a back door.

There was one merchant with a small snippet of blue in his hand who went up and down looking for a piece in the same color.

"But that is *our* color," I thought. "He is looking for an Upper High Royd piece; where is Jeremy?"

I scanned the market more closely and now caught sight of Jeremy and the blue piece, next to Mr. Gledhill with his three maroons. Just then the merchant with the blue pattern saw him too and stepped over to him and whispered, and the piece was sold and the merchant drew out his moneybag. While Jeremy was waiting for the money to be counted into his hand he looked up and caught my eye. I smiled at him, glad for Mr. Firth's sake that he had sold the piece. He gave me in reply a glance of such furious hatred that I was quite shaken, and hard put to it not to disgrace myself by speaking to Mr. Defoe. However, I managed to keep silence.

Presently the bell rang again, the doors were thrown open and merchants and clothiers all left the hall. We followed them out into the sunshine.

"I'll bid you farewell now, Tom," said Mr. Defoe. "I must go write this market down in my notes."

Indeed he seemed half away already in his mind, and hurried off toward the Rose and Crown. I was truly sorry to part from him.

Here I made what was perhaps a mistake. Having breakfasted so well at the inn with Mr. Defoe, I thought I need not eat again that day, and seeing all manner of agreeable things in the shops as I wandered about the town, I used my groat to buy a blue ribbon for little Gracie. This, as I say, was perhaps a mistake, for as the day went on I grew exceedingly hungry.

Halifax is a strange town, built at the foot of one great hill and lying up the slope of another rather less steep; the church is at the bottom, the gibbet at the top, the market cross midway between. I went down to the church, which is old and handsome enough (though not as large as Lavenham's) with very fine tall windows of plain glass, agreeably patterned by leads, and a most strange brightly painted wooden figure by the door, life size and dressed in quaint old-fashioned clothes. This figure, which gave me quite a start when I first entered the church, for I thought it a real man, was made to resemble a noted beggar who had lived nigh on two hundred years ago; it held a poorbox in front of it, in its hands. However, this Old Tristram, as they called him, is not really part of my story, except that, looking at him and at the church, and (I must confess) playing at ball with some lads I met around there, not only took my time but tired me out, hungry as I was, and made me long for a place to rest. As I had no money I could not enter an inn. So it was that I made my way to the Old Cock some hours before the time Jeremy had set. Mr. Gledhill's wagon stood in the yard with its shafts up—the horse would be in the stable—and two sacks of wool lying on it.

I climbed on to these sacks and pulling them about a little arranged a comfortable bed for myself. An ostler shouted at me, but I convinced him who I was and of my right to be there, on my master's wool, and he let me be. I curled myself up on the sacks, and what with hunger and fatigue and the excitement of the day and the hot sun beating down on me, I fell asleep.

I was wakened by being violently shaken by my shoulder. I started up and found myself gazing into the angry face of Mr. Gledhill.

"What are you doing here, Tom Leigh?" he said sternly.

"Waiting for Jeremy, sir," I said.

"Jeremy left long ago," said Mr. Gledhill.

"What? He has gone? He's left me? But how could he, when I am on your wagon?"

"You are not on any wagon, either mine or anybody else's," said Mr. Gledhill dryly.

I looked around, and saw to my amazement that I was in a dark corner of a stable, lying on straw, with Mr. Gledhill and the ostler gazing down at me.

"But I was on your wagon," I repeated stupidly, being but half awake.

"Aye, that's right, Mester Gledhill, he *was* on t' wagon,"

said the ostler. "I saw him there mysen, and bawled him out. Didn't I, lad? I bawled him out for lying on wool sacks, Mr. Gledhill, I did that."

I got to my feet and dusted the straw from my breeches.

"But how did I come into the stable?"

"Yon Jeremy must have carried thee in."

"But why should he do such a daft thing?"

"He's always against me, Mr. Gledhill," said I.

I own I had a great inclination to weep at this point, but lads of fourteen do not weep, so I choked down the lump in my throat, and said as boldly as I could:

"Well, no great harm has been done. It is but five miles, I can easily walk home."

"Tom Leigh, th'art either the daftest or the unluckiest boy I ever did encounter," said Mr. Gledhill, his expression softening somewhat. "Art sure, now, that tha wert not trying to break thy indentures and run away?"

"I am sure, Mr. Gledhill," said I firmly. "Where should I run to, in any case?"

"Well, there is that, to be sure," said Mr. Gledhill doubtfully.

"He were lying on wool on wagon," said the ostler with emphasis.

"I thank thee for thy good witness, friend," said I to him, "and I wish I could reward thee, but in truth I have nothing to give."

"Well—you had better ride pillion with me," said Mr. Gledhill in a kinder tone. "Find us a cushion, ostler. Here's for thy trouble."

So through the fading evening light I rode pillion behind Mr. Gledhill. It was dark when we reached Barseland; Jeremy was in Mr. Gledhill's stable, unharnessing the horse by candlelight.

"Why, Tom Leigh!" he exclaimed in a tone of pretended

concern as we entered. "Thank God you are safe! Whatever happened you, lad? Why did you not keep our meeting time, Tom? I went all over town seeking you!"

"Tom says he lay on the wool sacks on the wagon and fell asleep," said Mr. Gledhill drily.

"He weren't there when I came to t'wagon," said Jeremy, shaking his head.

"The ostler saw him there."

"Where did you find him, Mester Gledhill?"

"In a dark corner of the Old Cock stable. It was only by chance we found him. I needed a new lash to my whip and they hang there."

"Why did you go there, Tom lad?"

"I did not go there," said I stiffly.

"How did you get there, then?"

I was about to answer roughly: "You tell me!" when I thought to myself that I had the dark mile to Upper High Royd to walk, alone in his company, so I hung my head and said: "I do not know."

"Well, be off with you. I'm sick of the pair of you. Take Mr. Firth's wool, Jeremy," said Mr. Gledhill.

Jeremy took the pack on his back with my assistance.

"As for you, Tom," went on Mr. Gledhill, "if Mr. Firth is not in church tomorrow I shall ride up to see him and inquire into this matter."

"Nay, what's the need, Mr. Gledhill? Why get the lad into trouble?" said Jeremy smoothly. "He's back here safe and sound. He's never been to Halifax before, think on; he was all confused."

"Well," began Mr. Gledhill, hesitating. "I'll leave it for this time, Tom," he decided, "but it'll be long before I take you to Halifax again."

Jeremy and I went out into the dark.

"Art going to thank me for putting things straight with

Mester Gledhill, Tom?" said Jeremy in his smooth sneering tone.

"I thank you, Jeremy," said I. "I am much obliged."

This was a lie. For I did not believe a word he said. As I helped him to push the sack of wool across his back, I had just seen straw on the shoulder of his coat. Of course, he might have gained this straw while harnessing Mr. Gledhill's horse in the Old Cock stables. But I do not know how you get straw on your shoulder when you are harnessing a horse. Now if you are dragging a sleeping boy into a heap of straw, your shoulder might easily pick up a little.

I was very polite to Jeremy as we climbed the stony lane to Upper High Royd, but I kept behind him, and I was very thankful that his hands were occupied holding the sack of wool. That he hated me, that all his tricks on me were deliberate, I now was sure. But why he hated me so, I could not yet fathom.

7   Thieves in the Night

I OUGHT TO HAVE TOLD Mr. Firth at once the whole story of my sleeping on the wool sacks, but it was late when we reached Upper High Royd and he sent me straight up to bed—Sandy leaped up the stairs ahead of me, as he so often did, settled himself on my coverlet and mewed impatiently when I did not immediately lie down beside him.

In the morning at breakfast I offered the blue ribbon I had bought in Halifax to Gracie. Her eyes widened with pleasure, and suddenly before I knew what she was about she threw her arms about my neck and kissed me, standing on tiptoe to reach my cheek. I was much confused but somehow found I had put my arms around her—she is indeed a very sweet little girl. Mr. Firth laughed and seemed not displeased, his wife gave a thin smile, Jeremy in the background frowned as usual.

"Well now, enough, enough! You must be off to church," said Mr. Firth.

He himself stayed at home to rest his foot, so I had no chance to speak to him alone, and in the afternoon Harry carried me off to walk with him, so again I had no opportunity; then as the day wore on it began to seem less important. I was wrong there, however.

Mr. Firth having given his foot these several days' rest, it rapidly improved, so that he soon walked without limping and was able to get his foot in a stirrup though not to use the treadle. And Josiah having finished the threshing while we were in Halifax on Saturday, on Monday we all went back to our clothmaking business again. Jeremy finished a blue piece and Mr. Firth rode with it down to the fulling mill, so that by Wednesday afternoon Josiah and I stretched it out on the tenters to dry. The weather was still good, clear and breezy and sunny, though a little cold at night, so the piece would be well dry by Friday morning. Mr. Firth was pleased, as in spite of the harvesting and threshing and his lame foot, Upper High Royd would have sent a piece to market every Saturday throughout the summer.

On Thursday afternoon we had a call from the peddler. We were sitting at meat when his knock sounded, and I went to open the door. There he stood, spruce and neat as usual, with his bright green suit and his scarlet stockings.

"May I speak with Mistress Firth, if you please?" said he politely.

His pale plump face wore a look of concern.

"I'll be bound he has not brought those mittens," thought I as I called my mistress.

But I was wrong. He laid them on the top of his tray as Mrs. Firth approached. They were certainly handsome: gray with blue diamonds in lines, and the letters M.F. in blue on the wrist. Mrs. Firth exclaimed with pleasure, and even Mr. Firth, as he came to the door to pay for them, put his hand in his pocket without much reluctance. Gracie drew one mitten over her small hand.

"Why not a pair for the young lady?" said the peddler quickly.

"Well—can you take the measures?" said Mr. Firth. "Her hand is small, you know."

"Certainly, certainly," said the peddler, producing a tape measure from his pocket. "It will be a few weeks before I can bring them, sir; I expect to be up that way next week, but then they must be specially knitted, you understand. Now let me see: the letters are G.F., I think?"

I wondered a little that he knew Gracie's name so well, but no doubt, I thought, he had heard it said last time he called on us. He was shrewd, he missed nothing to his advantage—and even as I thought this, he gave me another instance of it. No sooner had he written down the measurements of Gracie's hand in a little book he carried than the look of concern dropped over his face like a curtain.

"But what am I about?" he said in a grieved tone. "Here am I foolishly plying my trade and forgetting my real errand." (Aye, and you will always forget an errand till you have done your own trade, I thought.) "I was at Clough End this morning, and I grieve to tell you, Mistress Firth, that I have ill news for you."

"My father?" cried Mrs. Firth, turning pale and clutching at her heart.

"Even so. He has a fever."

"But why have they not sent for me?" cried Mrs. Firth.

"There is talk of sending for you tomorrow," said the peddler soberly. "But if I were you, mistress—" He paused.

"Yes? Yes?"

"I would go today. After all, Mr. Sykes is elderly."

"He will be seventy come Michaelmas."

"And being widowed—"

"Oh, Stephen, I should never have left him."

"Nay, Meg," muttered Mr. Firth.

"Who is nursing him? How long has he had fever?"

"On these points I am not altogether certain," said the peddler thoughtfully.

"I must go to him," said Mrs. Firth with decision. "Stephen, I must go to him at once."

"And so you shall, love," said Mr. Firth heartily. "We'll set off now. Tom, go and saddle Bess. Put a pillion seat on her. Jeremy, if I'm not back by Friday night you must go to market yourself on Saturday. Mr. Gledhill will pass you into the hall."

"How shall I get the piece to Halifax, master?" whined Jeremy.

"Carry it on your shoulder," snapped Mr. Firth. "I've fetched many a piece that way myself. Now, Meg, as to Gracie—there's no need to trail the child all that way to a house of sickness."

"Mr. Sykes would no doubt like to have a last look at his granddaughter," put in the peddler. "Not that it will be his last, we hope," he added hastily as Mrs. Firth broke into a wail.

"She might catch the fever," said I.

"That's true enough, Tom."

"We can't leave her here," wailed Mrs. Firth.

"That's certain," agreed the peddler.

"Mrs. Gledhill will take her for a night or two," said Mr. Firth. "We'll leave her at Gledhill's on the way."

"I don't want to go to Gledhill's," cried Gracie, clinging to her father's arm.

It struck me that while I thought Mrs. Firth's devotion to her father rather foolish, Gracie's devotion to *her* father seemed natural. Mrs. Firth must have been a child once, I thought, surprised.

"Now, no silly work, Gracie," said Mr. Firth firmly. "Run off and help your mother to collect night-gear."

"Can I help at all?" offered the peddler.

"No, thankee. I'm obliged to you for the message," said Mr. Firth, giving him a florin.

"Then I'll be on my way. May I express the hope that you will find Mr. Sykes less ill than you fear," said the peddler.

He bowed politely and withdrew. We could see his scarlet stockings twinkling down the lane.

For the next half hour there was a great bustle. Mrs. Firth

was busy upstairs about clean linen for herself and Gracie; Mr. Firth changed into his market clothes and gave Jeremy instructions enough to last for a month. He hurried out to the tenters and felt the piece there.

"The weather's set fine for the night, I reckon," he said. "So you can leave the cloth out till morning, just to finish it off drying and stretching, like. Of course if the weather should change, bring it in."

"I will, master," said Jeremy obsequiously.

Meanwhile, I saddled Bess and brought her to the door.

"Hurry, Meg, hurry," cried Mr. Firth impatiently, pacing up and down the yard. "'Twill be dark before we reach Clough End if you don't make haste."

This was true enough, for we were now in September, the sun would set about half past six and to call at Mr. Gledhill's house in Barseland would take them a good twenty minutes out of their way, for he lived on the far side of the hill, facing toward Halifax.

At last they were off, Mrs. Firth riding Bess with Gracie pillion behind, and her husband leading the mare.

I felt downhearted as I saw them vanish round the turn of the lane, for the thought of spending some days alone with Jeremy was not agreeable to me. Sandy, who was lying on the wall in his usual sunny corner, seemed to feel the same; he turned his head and watched them with unusual attention, flicking the end of his tail, which hung over the wall, back and forth in a disturbed and dissatisfied fashion, and when I went over to have a word with him he gazed up at me from his great green eyes with an anxious pleading look and uttered a faint mew.

"Never mind, Sandy," said I, stroking his head. "She'll come back soon."

For it was Gracie to whom he gave his love—if indeed a

cat can truly love anyone but himself; they are haughty, withdrawn little animals.

"Dost mean to work today or not, Tom Leigh?" called Jeremy from the porch. "Just let me know."

However, Jeremy was very pleasant for the rest of the afternoon. While he was weaving he was silent, for the clack of the shuttle makes it difficult to hear voices, but when we paused for our drinking he became quite talkative, telling me all about Mrs. Firth's father and Clough End.

"No wonder she went there quick when she thought he was dying," he said. "She's his only daughter, his heiress, tha knows. She was after her own."

This seemed to me very unjust, for Mrs. Firth's concern for her father most clearly sprang from affection. But I said nothing, not wanting to provoke him, and he went on:

"It's a big place, is Clough End. They weave four or five pieces a week, and finish them themselves—raise them and crop them and all that."

"I know nothing of that end of clothmaking," said I.

"Tha knows nowt about owt, far as I can see," said Jeremy. "Sithee—wouldst like to try thy hand at weaving, Tom?"

"Not while Mr. Firth's away," said I.

"Afraid of breaking an end?" sneered Jeremy.

I said nothing, and after a moment he recovered his temper, and went on about Mr. Sykes.

"If he should die," he said, "Meg Firth would inherit Clough End, and she and Stephen would likely go and live there. How wouldst like that, eh, Tom?"

"I don't know," I said.

For indeed I was perplexed. To see a new place is always attractive, and in a bustling big house such as Clough End there might be other apprentices and I should be less lonely. But when I thought of leaving Upper High Royd, to my surprise I found my heart sink. I had grown fond of the place, the house and the beck and the trough, and Bess and Daisy and Sandy, and the heather moorland and the strong winds and the great hills rolling around. I did not wish to say anything to Jeremy about this, however.

"They won't sell Upper High Royd, though," said Jeremy, wagging his head. "They'll keep it for Gracie and the man she weds. Happen tha means to be him, eh, Tom Leigh?"

I was furious. That Gracie's name should be bandied about like this by a man like Jeremy put me in a real rage. I know I crimsoned. But I bit back the hot words which sprang to my lips, and picking up our mugs, went out of the workshop without saying a word. When I returned Jeremy was weaving, and I picked up my cards and we said no more.

The hours went on, the sun set, we gave up work and went downstairs. The wind began to rise and moan a little about the house. I made a good fire, fed Sandy, lighted the candles and got our supper, and we ate it very comfortably, though I was vexed that Jeremy took Mr. Firth's chair. There was no harm in it, perhaps, but I do not like to do behind folks' backs what you would not do before their faces. I let Sandy out—it was a fine night, with moonlight off and on; the moon almost full but with clouds chasing sometimes across its face.

When I came back to the hearth, I don't know why it was, but I felt suddenly uneasy. It was Jeremy's look, I think; as he lounged in Mr. Firth's chair he had such an air of triumph. There was no reason for this that I could see, but I was sure Jeremy had a reason, and it would be a bad one. It struck me how alone we were, how far from any other house, how long the night would be, how completely I was in Jeremy's power. He was not a strong-looking man, being thin and weedy in body, but his arms were like iron from throwing the shuttle all day long, and I had seen him carry a piece of cloth (which would weigh about twenty pounds) over his shoulder a mile uphill, without being in the least breathless or put about. His eyes gleamed as he looked at me sideways, and that sneering smile of triumph again curved his thin lips. I was just thinking how glad I was that Gracie was safe with Mr. Gledhill when he spoke.

"Be off with you to your bed, Tom Leigh."

I was glad enough to think of being out of his company, but I felt so sure everything he wished was evil that I resisted.

"It's early yet, Jeremy," I said, looking at the tall clock in the corner, which lacked a minute of nine.

"Happen. But I'm tired of the sight of you. Be off now."

"Sandy's still out."

"I'll let him in."

At this moment there came a not very loud crash from outside, as if the wind were banging an open door or window.

"I'll see to it," said Jeremy, starting up. "Now, art going to do as th'art told and get off to bed, or shall I make thee?"

His look was so ugly that I went straight for the stairs, pausing only to light my candle at the fire and pick up my two volumes of *Robinson Crusoe*. The clock struck nine as I put my foot on the step.

The wind was now howling about the house and causing all kinds of shuffling and cracking noises, but I lay comfortably in bed and read again about Crusoe's clothes: his high goatskin cap, his jacket and breeches of goatskin and his umbrella. I read about his fence, and his bed, and his grapes, and then reached the page when he suddenly came upon the print of a man's naked foot on the sandy shore of his island. Crusoe was terrified, and I am not ashamed to say that so was I. For such was Mr. Defoe's skill in the writing, that, though I had read it before, I felt all Crusoe's fright at finding this evidence of a man's presence on an island he had thought to be uninhabited. Crusoe fled to the house he had made for himself, in fear, and I turned uneasily in my bed and tried to keep my eyes from the shadows in the workshop corners.

It was just at this moment that I heard a very faint mew and a scratching at my door.

"It is Sandy," I said to myself, and felt quite comforted, and went to the door to let him in.

I raised the latch and pulled on the door. It did not yield. I gave a harder tug, but the door did not stir. I stooped and gazed at the handle and the space between door and jamb, and saw what was wrong: I was locked in. Just at this moment I heard a soft whisper from below, and the voice was the peddler's.

Then suddenly I saw the reason and nature of the thing, and could not imagine how I had been such a blind stupid fool as not to see it before. Jeremy and the peddler were the thieves who stole cloth from the tenters. Jeremy hated me because my presence crossed his plans; he wanted me out of the house; all his unkindness to me was to get rid of me, to maim me, to cause Mr. Firth to break my indentures, to drive me into running away. Jeremy's strange gestures at the tenters, the first day I came to Upper High Royd, had been warnings to the peddler to stay away. When the peddler came to the house the first time, Jeremy had pushed me downstairs so that he should see me and give up the plan of enticing Mr. and Mrs. Firth away from Upper High Royd that day—it was Jeremy who had sighed with relief when the peddler told Mrs. Firth her father was in good health.

For the message of his illness today was false without a doubt. (The peddler's urging that Gracie should be taken to see her grandfather showed his true motive: to get all the Firths out of the house.) The thieves had grown tired of waiting for me to be got rid of—or rather, the peddler and the other accomplice had grown tired; that was what they were all arguing about when Mr. Defoe had seen them at the Rose and Crown. Jeremy had made one last attempt to get rid of me, leaving me behind in the Old Cock stable, hoping I would run away. But when I turned up—how furious Mr. Gledhill's rescue of me must have made him—he decided to risk the danger of my presence and lock me in. The tenters were out of sight of the workshop windows. And the peddler, a man with a licence to sell, always traveling about, was just the person to arrange the cloth's sale. Yes, it was all clear; everything that had perplexed me about Jeremy was now explained.

And here was I, alone in the house with two thieves, Mr. Firth away, his cloth under his apprentice's care. If I was to be his "good and faithful servant," as my indentures said, I *must* try to prevent the theft.

The mewing at my door had now ceased; Sandy no doubt had given me up and gone away.

I dressed, as quickly and quietly as I was able, putting on my jacket to cover the white of my shirt, but leaving off my clogs, as they would clatter on the stones of the yard.

The house door closed softly. I listened with all my ears, and thought I heard quiet footsteps going toward the far end of the house.

But there was only one way to make sure. I waited a few moments to give Jeremy and the peddler time to be out of earshot; then I unbolted the taking-in doors and swung them back. I unwound the rope and let it slide over the pulley till the hook was nearly at the ground, then fastened it round the staples. I drew the rope toward me, grasped it firmly with both hands, swung out and descended it hand below hand.

I cannot pretend that this descent was comfortable or that I performed it well. Each time I had to move one hand I was afraid of falling, never having done anything like this before. To avoid this fear, I tried at one moment to slide down the rope, but this took the skin off my palms and left them very sore. For a moment I hung helpless in mid-air, sweating—I do not deny it—with fear. At last I found that if I clasped the rope between my feet much weight was taken off my hands, and after that I did pretty well, except that I caught one foot in the curve of the hook when I reached it and could not at first get free. I fell to the ground and hopped about, following the rope as it swayed, but at length managed to release myself and stood safe on the ground in my stockinged feet.

I crept round the back of the house and clambered very softly—this is not easy on these mortarless West Riding walls —over the wall at the side of the tentercroft. The moon had escaped from its clouds and was riding high, shedding a bright silver light over house and fields. The scene was very beautiful but somehow rather eerie, because of the deep black shadows cast by buildings and walls. For one of these black shadows, however, I was very grateful; it stretched along the side of the tentercroft wall and enabled me to crawl along toward the tenters, unseen. I kept my face down, so that the moonlight should not shine white upon it, as I approached. Yes, there they were: Jeremy unhooking the cloth, the peddler standing by; each grumbling at the other.

"Can't you hurry, man?" said the peddler. "In this moonlight we can be seen a mile away."

"It were you who chose to do it tonight," growled Jeremy.

"I was tired of waiting."

"I were only trying to get rid o' that nuisance of a lad."

"He's perfectly safe locked up in the workshop. He'll help to support your own tale of not having heard any sounds in the night. Come, man, make haste!"

"If you want more haste you can help to make it," snarled Jeremy. "Take your coat off and give me a hand."

"Oh, very well," said the peddler, shrugging. "Where shall I start work, eh?"

"Go back to the beginning and take cloth off the top nails —I've taken it off the bottom row, back there."

The peddler stepped toward me, so that for a moment my heart was in my mouth. I buried my head in my arms on the ground and lay absolutely still for what seemed the longest moment of my life. I heard soft shuffling sounds as the peddler took off his coat, and then a clink—the brass buttons, I guessed, had struck against the wall as he threw the coat aside. This clinking sounded very near, and I own I was afraid.

"Ouch!" cried the peddler of a sudden.

I ventured to raise my head a very little. Having often helped Jeremy or Josiah to take a piece off the tenters and knowing its difficulties, I could not help being amused at the peddler's lack of skill—he had torn one of his fingers on the tenter nails. He had this finger in and out of his mouth, shaking it and sucking it, and was dancing with the pain, and loosing off a string of oaths when his mouth was free.

"Make less noise, will you?" said Jeremy. "And pay more heed. It's going to take us all night to get twelve yards off, if you go on like this."

"We'll take the whole eighteen yards; it's not worth stealing less."

"It'll look more natural like to take twelve."

"But more dangerous. They'll have some left, then, for a pattern."

"I say twelve."

"Don't forget," said the peddler smoothly, "that it was I who arranged the sale, Jeremy Oldfield."

"I could ha' done that mysen."

"But you didn't."

"Howd thy gab," said Jeremy viciously. "And get to work. Or by gum, I'll make thee."

"There is no need to lose your temper, my dear Jeremy," said the peddler in his smoothest tones.

I do not know whether it was their hateful talk, or the remembrance of the many vile ways in which Jeremy had tried to get rid of me from Upper High Royd, or the cunning of the peddler's skillful lie about Mrs. Firth's father—I do not know, I say, what put it into my head; but I was wearing my jacket and the scissors Gracie had given me were in my inner pocket as always, and the peddler's full-skirted coat lay only a few inches from my head. I drew it softly into the deep black shadow and turned it partly over, and I took out my scissors, and pinched up the lining in the fold of the back skirt of the peddler's coat and cut out a small piece like this.

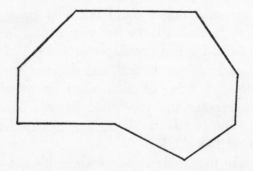

Just as I began I remembered Sir Henry cutting my indentures in a zigzag line, and I remembered the reason he had given me for doing so, and I cut the edges of my piece of the peddler's lining zigzag too. I shall never forget the shape.

I tucked the scissors and the piece of lining firmly into my pocket, and I gathered my courage, and then I stood up and stepped out of the black shadow into the silver moonlight.

It would be a lie to pretend that I was not afraid. I was

so much afraid that my voice shook and my stomach seemed to fall out of me as I said:

"What are you about, Jeremy?"

Jeremy turned and saw me. His face contorted into a grimace so evil that it haunts me yet in my dreams, and with a scream of rage he hurled himself upon me. The force of his charge bore me to the ground; he held me down with his left hand and began to beat my head with his clenched right fist. I kicked at his ankles; my left hand being free I caught his wrist and tried to throw him off, and we rolled over and over on the ground. His right arm was so strong (from continually throwing the shuttle) that I could not retain it for long in my grasp, but I pushed it back upward as hard as I was able. In this posture my own left arm was at full stretch, exposed to the view of the peddler, whose smooth face I could see from time to time; he stood to one side of the fight, not moving, his eyebrows raised sardonically. At this point he raised his right foot, and with a smile of pleasure kicked my forearm hard.

I heard the bone crack, and could not prevent a cry of pain. My arm dropped useless at my side, and Jeremy's face above me grinned with satisfaction.

"Don't kill him, Jeremy," said the peddler smoothly, bending over us.

"Why not? I should have finished him off in the stream at Mearclough and then we wouldn't have had all this bother," said Jeremy.

He leaned on my broken arm with all his weight, so that the pain was agonizing, and again I gave a cry.

"Now you've told him about Mearclough you'll be obliged to kill him," said the peddler, in a tone of slight vexation, as if the matter in question were a broken teacup or something of that kind. "Well, it's no matter. We'll leave the body here. He will appear to have died defending Mr. Firth's tenters against unknown thieves—you must shed a tear and speak well of him tomorrow, Jeremy."

Jeremy replied to this with an oath.

"Give me a stone to finish him off," he said.

The peddler moved aside to search for one. I made a tremendous effort—probably the last of my life, I thought, but one should die fighting—and rolled to one side, and shouted:

"Help! Help!" at the top of my voice.

I did not think, of course, that there could be any help for me nearer than a couple of miles, but there I was wrong, for as the peddler stooped to pick up a stone, something flew through the air from the wall and landed on Jeremy's shoulders. It was Sandy, who must have escaped from the house when the thieves opened the door to go to the tenters. Spitting, biting, clawing, he vented all his hate, and it was now Jeremy's turn to scream with pain.

"Get this cat off me, blast you!" he yelled.

"I can't abide cats," said the peddler, standing well back.

Jeremy put up his hands to seize hold of the cat. My arms being thus released, I got my right hand against his chin and pushed with all my might. He was obliged to draw back or have his neck broken; my upper body was free, I rolled myself out from under him and sprang for the wall.

How I got over it with one arm useless, I do not know; partly perhaps I vaulted, partly jumped, partly scrambled, partly just fell; at any rate I found myself in the harvested oats field, and rushed down it headlong. The stubble was hard on my stockinged feet, but at least it was kinder than the stones of the lane. There was no shadow here; the moon just beamed relentlessly down the field. I hurled myself over the wall at the foot of the field, and lay in the shadow there for a moment to decide what I should do next.

The shouts and mewing from the tentercroft had now died

away—what had happened to poor Sandy, I wondered? Cats have a great turn of speed, I thought hopefully, thanking Sandy for coming to the sound of my voice. He had always hated Jeremy. Think about yourself, not Sandy, I told myself, but I could not at first take my thoughts away from the cat. At last, however, I seemed to collect my breath and my thoughts; I became conscious of the fierce pain in my left arm, and managed with my right hand to pull my left between the buttons of my jacket to hold the broken forearm in place.

Where should I go for help? Mr. Gledhill's was the obvious answer; Gracie was there and she would believe my tale. To do that I should have to cross the lane leading down from Upper High Royd to Barseland, which lay in full moonlight to my right, where it joined the road, and even as I thought this I heard footsteps coming down the lane. As they approached I could hear Jeremy cursing the wounds he had received from Sandy's claws, and reproaching the peddler for not having come more quickly to his rescue, while the peddler replied soothingly in his mincing tones. They reached the foot of the lane and stood there, talking. The peddler, I saw through a chink in the wall, had donned his coat, which did not surprise me, for indeed the wind blew chill.

"Where the hell will t'lad have gone?" grumbled Jeremy.

"That is for you to say," said the peddler.

"How should I know?"

"Give it a little thought."

"Well—happen to Gledhill's. Gracie's there and she's sweet on him. She'll believe owt he says."

"Then we mustn't let him get there."

"That's right. We shall have to finish him off this time. Pity we didn't do it that night in Mearclough."

"'We'? It was you who struck the boy with a stone, Jeremy."

"Tha wert as deep in it as I was, peddler," said Jeremy in an ugly threatening tone. "Nay, deeper!"

"We were in it together," said the peddler smoothly.

"Aye—and don't thee forget it."

"I'm not likely to do so while this tiresome boy is roaming round. He came down the oats field. He must be somewhere hereabout. Let me see, now. Gledhill's place is over to the right. We want to scare him out into the moonlight. Then we'll finish him off, and you go back to Upper High Royd and sleep the sleep of the just, and I'll be off to you know where with the cloth. Remember, Jeremy, you haven't seen me since this afternoon."

"I'm non a fool, tha knows. But how can we get hold of Tom?"

"Oh, we'll soon smoke out dear Tom," said the peddler, laughing.

Suddenly there rang through the moonlit air a strong clear cry:

"Keep to the left, Jeremy! He's over there!"

I shuddered, and the hair at the base of my neck prickled, as I heard these words. *Keep to the left* was the cry that had sent my father to his death; and the voice was the same voice which had cried the words that night in Mearclough. It was the peddler's voice; his real voice, let loose from the shrill primness he usually affected.

I sprang up and turned to the right, for my natural impulse was to go in a direction away from that urged on Jeremy, and I believed the peddler had in truth seen me; but luckily my knowledge of his character, of his lying, scheming ways, served me well; to frighten me into turning right was that clever devil's intention. I halted, then ran away to the left as hard as I could.

They heard me brushing through the grass.

"He's off!" cried Jeremy.

"After him!" cried the peddler.

"After him thysen—I've had all the knocks I want from that lad tonight," grumbled Jeremy.

"Don't be a fool, Jeremy—we don't want him to reach Gledhill's."

"He's running away from Gledhill's."

"All the better. After him, you fool!"

Although all this was spoken very quickly, still Jeremy's hesitation gave me a few yards' start, and as Mr. Gledhill had noticed I had grown a good deal in the last few months and had long legs. I outdistanced them at first, but then uncertainty—and perhaps the pain of my arm, which hurt excruciatingly when jolted—began to slow my steps. Where could I go for help? I could not now reach Mr. Gledhill without turning and passing my pursuers. I tried to think how I could make a wide enough circle to avoid them; it must be a route where there was shadow to hide me, for the moon was still piercingly bright. I thought longingly of the great bushes round Sir Henry's mansion—and that of course gave me my answer: Harry! Harry would shelter me. The high wall of Sir Henry's estate began on the far side of the road; I rushed across, got a handhold on the wall and threw myself over.

Jeremy and the peddler saw me in the moonlight and gave a shout and hurried their steps, and my crash into the bushes broke enough twigs to be heard a mile away, but I wriggled along beneath the bushes as fast as I could. I thought quickly: Jeremy could climb the wall but would hardly dare to do so, for gentlemen are not fond of laboring men who climb their walls in the middle of the night; the peddler was too plump and lazy for climbing; they would have to go round to the great gates. I had a moment to gain the house.

I came to the edge of the bushes, and scratched up some dirt, and ran across the courtyard and threw a handful of dirt up at what I remembered to be Harry's window. I was in moonlight here again, and I thought I heard distant exclamations behind me, as though Jeremy and the peddler were at the gates and had seen me. There was no sign from Harry's window. I threw at it again. There was still no sign, and I heard the squeak of the gate as it swung open. In despair I snatched up a pebble which lay beside my foot, and threw it with all my might, so that it struck sharply on the glass pane. Then at last one of the mullioned windows opened and Harry leaned out.

"They have broken my arm and mean to kill me, Harry," I cried softly. "For God's sake let me in."

Harry's face changed and he turned aside. For one awful moment I thought he meant not to help me and I was doomed. Then he was at the window again and threw down one end of a big greatcoat.

"I've tied its sleeve here. Get hold of the end and help yourself up."

"I have only one arm, Harry, the other's broken," I said despairingly.

"There are toe holds in the wall. I've often climbed it," said Harry. "Put your foot there, see—and then here."

I did his bidding, and he hauled me upward on the coat, which I clutched in one hand. There came a moment when my senses reeled so with pain that I feared I could not keep my grip. But Harry seized my hand and then my arm and pulled me up and I got my head through the window opening. The casement looked very narrow.

"I shall never get my shoulders through," I thought despairingly.

But Harry turned my body so that my shoulders lay up and down to the casement instead of across, and he pushed his hands into my armpits and heaved, and suddenly I fell through the window onto the floor of Harry's bedchamber. As I fell I knocked my broken arm against the dressing table to which he had tied the greatcoat. The pain was so acute that I groaned and fainted.

8   My Word Is Doubted

THIS FAINTING OF MINE was the most unfortunate event (save my father's death, of course) in my life, because it caused delay, and this delay gave the thieves time to appear to shed some of their guilt. For Harry tried to revive me but could not, so fetched a servingman, who likewise could not; it was only then, when they began to fear I was dead, that Harry went for Sir Henry. I was brought to my senses somewhat ungently by the jar to my arm as Robert and another man of Sir Henry's lifted me up onto Harry's bed. I opened my eyes and saw above me in the candlelight a figure which at first I did not recognize, but presently perceived to be Sir Henry in a long gown and without his wig. Harry too was in a nightgown, and the two men were in shirt sleeves, without their livery coats, so that at first I was quite perplexed, and gazed at them all dreamily. Then the candles flickered in the draught from the open window and I remembered my climb into Harry's room and its cause and I sat up and cried:

"Catch them! Sir Henry, send after them! They are stealing the cloth from Mr. Firth's tenters! Jeremy! The peddler! They are stealing the cloth!"

"Who is Jeremy?" asked Sir Henry.

"Jeremy Oldfield—he is Mr. Firth's journeyman weaver, who lives with us in the house."

"Journeyman weavers do not usually live in their masters' houses," said Sir Henry.

"Jeremy has no kin nigh at hand with whom to live. The

peddler is a man who has been to the house before, he is a friend of Jeremy's—"

"How do you know that?"

"Mr. Defoe saw them talking together in the inn."

"Well, well, come to the point," said Sir Henry impatiently.

"This afternoon the peddler came to Upper High Royd with a message for Mrs. Firth that her father was ill. Then Mr. and Mrs. Firth set off at once to visit him, and took Miss Gracie down to Mr. Gledhill's, so that the house was empty save for Jeremy and me. I think the message was false, meant to empty the house."

"Why? Did the peddler remain at Upper High Royd?"

"No, sir, he left at once, but returned after dark."

I went on to tell how Jeremy had sent me up to bed; how the cat's mewing had sent me to try my door and I had found myself locked in; how I had escaped by the taking-in doors—Harry's eyes gleamed with pleasure at this—how I had crept in shadow to the tenters and watched Jeremy and the peddler taking off the cloth, how I had challenged them.

"Bravo!" cried Harry.

How Jeremy had sprung on me and knocked me down and we had fought on the ground together.

"And then the peddler kicked my arm and broke it," I concluded.

Sir Henry exclaimed and stepping to the bedside took my forearm very carefully in his hands.

"Yes, it is broken," he said. "Heark'ee, Tom," he went on after a moment's thought, "I will send down to the valley for a surgeon to attend your arm, but meanwhile my groom here, Robert, will tie it for you—he has set a dog's leg, there is not much difference between that and a man's arm."

"But the tenters, sir!" I cried. "They are stealing the cloth from Mr. Firth's tenters!"

"Are you sure you did not dream all this, Tom? And wake up startled and rush from the house, and break your arm tumbling over the wall?"

"Send to Upper High Royd, and see! You will find the cloth torn off the tenters, and the taking-in doors open! Mr. Swain had cloth stolen, too, do you not remember, Sir Henry?"

"Yes, that is true. And others also. You tell a wild tale, but it must be investigated. James," he said to the older servingman, "saddle a horse and go to Mr. Gledhill. Present my compliments and tell him Tom's story, and say I think he should proceed at once to Upper High Royd, and find Jeremy Oldfield and this peddler, and bring them here to me to answer these allegations. We had better have the clerk present, too, to record their depositions."

"Oh, make haste, make haste," I cried. "They will be miles away by now!"

"Nonsense," said Sir Henry. "They have no horses."

"They will have hidden the cloth. They are stealing the cloth from Mr. Firth's tenters," I wailed.

By this time my voice had grown weak and my speech uncertain, for I was faint again with pain and fatigue.

"I think the lad hath a fever," said Robert.

"It may well be so, and these may be ravings. But yet we must examine into the matter," said Sir Henry. His voice was cold and unfriendly, and he made to leave the room. "Tell me, Tom Leigh," he said: "If what you say is true, and these men attacked you—"

"It was only Jeremy, sir. The peddler stood by and watched—oh! and he put on his coat," I cried, remembering. "Sir Henry, I—"

"How did you escape from Jeremy?"

"Sandy the cat sprang at him—he hates Jeremy—he clawed the back of Jeremy's neck and Jeremy took his hands from me in order to defend himself, and I rolled clear. But the peddler stood aside—he cannot touch a cat—he put on his coat—he had thrown aside his coat before. And I cut this," I said eagerly, trying to reach inside my jacket. "Harry, help me! I have a piece of lining I cut from the peddler's coat. He threw off his coat beside the tenter, to help Jeremy, and he tore his finger, and I cut a piece of lining—"

"Robert," Sir Henry nodded to the groom.

The man put his hand inside my jacket and fumbled for the pocket; this was agony for my arm, but I endured greater agony in my mind when it seemed for a moment as if he could not find the piece of stuff. However, presently his hand fell on it and he drew it out and passed it to Sir Henry.

"A jagged piece," said Sir Henry thoughtfully, fingering it. "Why did you cut it this strange shape, Tom?"

His tone was kinder, and I felt heartened.

"It was because of the indentures, sir," I said. "You said —you cut a jagged edge—so that—only that one piece would fit the other." I sighed despairingly, unable to find the right words.

"I understand your meaning, Tom," said Sir Henry. "You shall confront these men when I have them in my hands, and we shall see which of you are rogues. Put the stuff back within his coat, Robert. Bring the piece of lining with you when you are summoned, Tom. But keep it hidden and say nothing of it till I call on you."

He left the room, and Robert began the painful process of setting my arm. Harry helped me through this by sitting beside me and offering me his hand to grip; I set my teeth and clung to it with all my power and managed not to cry out, though I was hard put to it and sweat rolled down my forehead.

When it was over and my arm strapped across my body I lay back on the pillows for a while and the groom brought me a drink of wine—very sour stuff I thought it but it restored my spirits to some extent. The groom went away, leaving Harry and me alone together, but we hardly knew what to say to each other and sat silent, grinning occasionally. I think I slept a little from exhaustion. Then the groom came back and said:

"You're to come now, Tom Leigh."

I rolled off the bed with Harry's help, and he took my right arm—Robert made to hold me on the left but I could not bear to be touched on that side—and helped me down the stairs and along the passage, and touched my shoulder gently and said:

"Good luck, Tom."

He opened the door and I stumbled in.

It was a kind of repetition of what had happened when I was apprenticed, and for a moment I felt confused, uncertain whether it was then or now. Then I saw Jeremy and the peddler standing before Sir Henry's table, with Mr. Swain and Mr. Gledhill at their shoulders, and the back of my neck prickled, and I remembered all that had happened that night, and my anger rose hot and strong and I held myself firmly. It was just coming dawn, and the light was chill and wan. Jeremy looked dirty and hangdog, with blood about his shirt collar, but the peddler was spruce and jaunty, as usual.

"Oh, Tom, Tom!" said he, shaking his head at me. "Oh, Tom Leigh! To think that you should come to this! That a lad like you should set about to rob so good a master! That I should see you engaged in a felony!"

I was so astonished that I gaped at him, speechless.

"A felony, you think?" said Sir Henry quietly.

He was dressed now, and wearing his wig, and looked extremely grave and like a magistrate, and spoke in a much more severe and weighty tone than on the day of my apprenticeship. The peddler seemed somewhat taken aback, and said hastily in his mincing tones:

"I am unfamiliar with legal terms, your worship."

"Humph!" said Sir Henry.

It seemed to me that he thought just the reverse, namely that the peddler was altogether too familiar with legal terms for a man who had never crossed the law, and that the peddler perceived this.

"Now, peddler, let us hear your story of the night's happenings. First, your name, your place of abode, your occupation."

"My name is Anthony Dyce. I have no permanent place of abode save my brother's house in Cheapside, London. I hold a peddler's licence."

"Show it to me."

The peddler handed a sheet of paper to Sir Henry, who examined it carefully.

"It is in order. Now, your story."

"With great respect, Sir Henry, would it not be well to hear the boy's tale first, so that—"

"So that he can fit his tale to mine," I thought angrily, but I said nothing.

"Don't keep me waiting, my man," said Sir Henry shortly.

"As your worship pleases. Well, earlier in the day I was at Upper High Royd and received an order for a pair of woolen mittens for the young lady of the house."

"Gracie," put in Jeremy.

The peddler scowled at him.

"They were to be knitted to include her name—either her name or the first letters of her name," said the peddler smoothly. "Later in the day when I came to reflect on the matter, I could not remember which it was to be. So I returned to Upper High Royd to make inquiry."

"On your first visit to Upper High Royd today, did you bring a message to Mrs. Firth that her father was ill?"

"Not a message," replied the peddler. "Oh, no; not a *message*. It was common talk in Almondbury, and as such I repeated it."

"Mr. Firth and his wife and daughter then left the house as a consequence of your repeating it?"

"They left the house," agreed the peddler with an air of being very particular as to the truth of all he said.

"You returned later, knowing they had left the house?"

"I returned later to inquire about the mittens."

"But there would be nobody there able to answer you?"

"Jeremy and the boy were both present when the mittens were ordered."

"So far your tale is weak," said Sir Henry sternly. "Continue."

"Jeremy and I were sitting by the fire, engaged in a few minutes' talk about the mittens, when we heard a noise outside. We ran out, and saw the boy Thomas Leigh pulling off a piece of cloth from the tenters. Jeremy sprang forward and bade him desist; the boy struck him and ran away. We followed, and to our astonishment tracked him to your mansion."

"How did Jeremy Oldfield obtain those long scratches on the back of his neck and head?"

"Ah, that was the cat, which sprang on him. Tom Leigh, I fear, set the cat on to Jeremy by hissing to it."

"You did not assist in the pulling of the cloth from the tenters?"

"I, sir? Certainly not."

"And you, Jeremy Oldfield, did you pull the cloth from the tenters with intent to steal it?"

"No, it were t'lad," said Jeremy uneasily, shifting from one foot to the other.

"You, Anthony Dyce, do you affirm you did not kneel beside the tenters and help to pull off the cloth?"

"Yes, indeed. I have no skill with tenters," said the peddler, smiling.

Sir Henry looked at me.

"They locked me in the workshop. I climbed out by the taking-in place and saw them both taking the cloth off the nails of the tenter," said I.

"Mr. Gledhill," said Sir Henry. "You proceeded to Upper High Royd tonight at my request. What did you find there?"

"The tenters were bare of cloth, the taking-in doors were open."

"Open?" exclaimed the peddler and Jeremy together. The peddler gave Jeremy a very sour glance.

"Open," repeated Mr. Gledhill firmly. "Jeremy Oldfield was in bed, however, apparently asleep."

"I *was* asleep," said Jeremy peevishly.

"Was the door of the workshop locked, as Thomas Leigh states?"

"No."

"Ah, Tom," said the peddler, shaking his head at me: "How could you tell such shocking lies?"

"Jeremy could easily have unlocked it on his return to Upper High Royd," said Mr. Gledhill.

"So that proves nothing," said Sir Henry thoughtfully.

"Nobody denies that Tom Leigh climbed out of the house by the taking-in place," said the peddler swiftly. "He did so to avoid being seen by Jeremy and myself, no doubt."

"I saw you both taking the cloth from the tenters," I repeated. "It was moonlight and I hid in the shadow of the wall."

Jeremy moistened his lips uneasily, but the peddler gave an airy laugh.

"I suppose you recognized me by my scarlet stockings?"

"No," I said. I was surprised by my own answer, but it was the truth. I had not noticed the peddler's stockings that night until now. I felt perplexed and cast down, but then I saw a frown cross the peddler's face; he was vexed by my answer; why?

"They would not show scarlet in the moonlight!" I cried.

"What a clever lad you are, Tom Leigh! Altogether too cunning for your own good," sneered the peddler.

"I simply tell the truth," I cried, turning back to Sir Henry. "I challenged the pair of them, Jeremy sprang at me and knocked me down, while I was trying to hold him off the peddler kicked my arm and broke it."

"Tut tut tut! Such lies from one so young!"

"The boy was always a fighter," muttered Mr. Swain disagreeably.

"You deny the attack, peddler? Am I to take it, then, that the boy's arm was broken in the struggle with Jeremy Oldfield?" inquired Sir Henry shrewdly.

"Nay! It wasn't me," began Jeremy.

The peddler, as I saw but I think the others did not, kicked him sharply on the ankle with his heel, and he fell silent.

"Mr. Swain, I asked you to search for the peddler and bring him to me," said Sir Henry. "Where did you find him?"

"In the Fleece Inn, drinking with the host," said Mr. Swain. "At least, that was the appearance. He seemed, however, a trifle breathless."

"That was the ale," cackled the peddler.

"Did he offer any resistance to coming to the magistrate?"

"None at all. He jested all the way here, but tried to pick my brains as to what had happened."

"Anthony Dyce, remove your coat," said Sir Henry suddenly.

The peddler stared.

"Take off your coat!" thundered Sir Henry. "Or shall I call my men to take it from you?"

The peddler held up his hand.

"Do not have me touched, I beg. Since you desire it, Sir Henry, I will remove my coat myself."

Slowly and nonchalantly, with elegant gestures, he removed the coat.

"Spread it out on the table, with the lining on the outside."

With a graceful turn of his hand the peddler threw it down as requested.

"Tom," said Sir Henry, beckoning me.

I stepped forward, drew the piece of lining from within my jacket, and placed it over the hole which showed plainly in the skirt of the peddler's coat. It was not quite easy to do with one hand, but after a little fumbling I managed. I rejoiced to see how the piece fitted into the hole exactly, and matched the rest of the lining in silky texture and green color.

"Where and when did you obtain this piece of the lining of the peddler's coat?"

"Beside Mr. Firth's tenters—the peddler threw off his coat and knelt down to help Jeremy take off the cloth—I cut the piece out with my scissors," I said, drawing them from my pocket.

There was a moment's pause, then the peddler broke into a roar of laughter.

"You young devil! I never heard a better story!" he cried.

"How do you explain the jagged piece which fits your coat?"

"Nay, how should I know?" said the peddler cheerfully. "I suppose I may have laid my coat aside in the house while talking with Jeremy, because of the heat of the fire. There was a big fire on the hearth, I seem to remember."

"That's right," said Jeremy—and for once he spoke truth.

"You think the boy could have come downstairs and cut a piece out of your coat, under your very nose?"

"I would not put anything beyond the reach of that young devil," said the peddler. "He is as clever as a load of monkeys."

"Where is the blue cloth, then?" said I, stubbornly.

"You tell us where you have hidden it," laughed the peddler.

"Sir Henry, the cloth was still partly on the tenters when I ran away," I said. "And when Mr. Gledhill reached Upper High Royd, it was all gone. There were eighteen yards. I have never carried a whole piece of cloth, sir."

"So you say," said Mr. Swain.

"Where would the boy sell the cloth? The peddler has every opportunity to sell it," said Mr. Gledhill.

"Well, gentlemen, what do you think of the evidence?" said Sir Henry.

"It is either those two or the boy. Both boy and peddler were in Barseland the night my cloth was stolen," said Mr. Swain.

"Eighteen yards, think on, Swain," said Mr. Gledhill.

"Aye, the whole piece."

"The boy could not have carried it far."

"True. But he could have hidden it."

"But there is the piece of lining, Sir Henry," persisted Mr. Gledhill.

"We shall see when Stephen Firth returns, whether the message taking him away was false or no," said Sir Henry.

"If it was false, then I say the peddler was guilty," said Mr. Gledhill stoutly. "And if he is guilty, Jeremy Oldfield is his accomplice."

"It was not a message," said the peddler. "Just something I had heard. As for the boy's arm, he attacked Jeremy Oldfield and I defended him. If the arm got broken, it is his own fault."

"The boy was always ready at fighting," repeated Mr. Swain.

"Hold Oldfield and the peddler in custody, and send a messenger to Firth," decided Sir Henry. "I will keep the boy here till Firth returns."

"He looks to have a fever," observed Mr. Gledhill. "His cheeks are scarlet."

"That may come from guilt and shame," said Mr. Swain. "No!" I cried.

But Sir Henry nodded sternly to me to go.

I stumbled out. Harry and Robert were waiting for me beyond the door, indeed I think they had been listening to what went on before Sir Henry. They helped me upstairs and put me to bed in a pleasant small chamber next to Harry's, and Robert lighted a fire and fetched a hot warming pan for the bed, while Harry helped me out of my clothes, gently and carefully.

But I could hardly mumble a word of thanks; I hung my head and my voice choked in my throat; my heart was almost broken to know that a Justice of the Peace, a Constable and an Overseer, all men of high repute, doubted my word.

9 The Third Accomplice

M R. SWAIN WAS WRONG in thinking that I colored with shame, but Mr. Gledhill was right in guessing that my flushed face might spring from fever. Whether it was from my broken arm, or the beating from Jeremy, or my headlong rush down the hill, or the drink of wine, to which I myself ascribed it, or whether it sprang from my mind's torment, I do not know; but that very night I fell into a high fever, and dreamed and raved till, Robert said, it was pitiful to hear me.

I saw Jeremy's face black with fury, coming closer and closer, till I screamed that he should not touch me, and then the peddler laughing and twitching his eyebrows sardonically, and then cloth rippling off the tenters to the ground. This last seemed to distress me most, said Robert who had the task of watching beside me; I continually cried out about cloth and tenters and Mr. Firth, and then sat up in bed and said very seriously: "I must stop the thieves," and made to throw aside the bedclothes and struggled vehemently when Robert pressed me back into the pillows. Sir Henry, I am told, came often to look at me and perhaps my ravings helped to support my innocence in his mind, I do not know. Of all this time I am ignorant, save that this confused medley of tenters and faces seemed to roll around in my aching head for a long, long time, and then it seemed to fade a little and move less rapidly, and then it ceased and everything was blank, and then I heard a heavy sigh, and I opened my eyes, and there sitting at my bedside was Mr. Firth. His round pleasant face was quite long and heavy.

"Oh, Mr. Firth," I said at once: "How glad I am to see you!"

His face brightened.

"Why, Tom!" he said. "Hast come to thy senses, lad? Art not about to die, after all?"

"I don't want to die, Mr. Firth," I said weakly, for indeed I did not know whether I had the strength to stay alive.

"That's a good lad, Tom!" said Mr. Firth heartily.

"When can I come back to Upper High Royd, master?"

"When you are well enough."

"Can I come back today?"

"You are not fit, Tom."

"Tomorrow, then?"

"Tom," said Mr. Firth uneasily, "Sir Henry, I fear—that is, I fear—I fear he will not let you go."

"Not let me go!"

"You see, Tom, there has been such a to-do about this affair. All Barseland is in a lather about it—nay, the whole parish of Halifax! They talk about it day and night! *You* accuse Jeremy and the peddler, and *they* accuse *you*, and folk are taking sides. Some blame Sir Henry for putting Jeremy and the peddler into gaol, you know, and say it is a good thing you are here under lock and key; if he were to let you go, there would be a great outcry. My stolen cloth cannot be found, you see, though it's been looked for high and low; and yet, Jeremy and the peddler did not leave Barseland that night after the robbery."

"But was not the peddler's message to Mrs. Firth, from her father, false?" I asked, astounded.

"Aye, it was—in a way. When we reached Clough End Mr. Sykes had gone to Huddersfield that morning and had not yet returned. We came straight home."

"The peddler's message was false, then—a decoy. To get you and Mrs. Firth out of the house. Surely that proves they meant to rob you!"

"Why, you see," said Mr. Firth uncomfortably, "Mr. Sykes is a man who often has a touch of discomfort in his digestion, and being the most important man in the place, he is much talked about, and the peddler says he heard of Mr. Sykes's illness only in an inn, it was not a message, he says; my wife just chose to take it so."

I groaned.

"And then, you see, Tom," continued Mr. Firth, "you remember you said Mr. Defoe had seen the peddler and Jeremy together one night shortly before the robbery, in the Rose and Crown in Halifax? Well, Sir Henry wrote to Mr. Defoe in London."

"But what difference would that make?" I asked.

"It would be conspiracy, you see, if they planned it beforehand. Besides, they'd denied knowing each other until that day. Well, for long enough Sir Henry had no answer, and Barseland folk began to wonder—"

"Whether I had lied," I said bitterly.

"Well, they began to wonder. But now, Tom, you may take heart. Today a letter has come from Mr. Defoe, and it's a proper deposition, like, a statement made on oath before magistrates. Three men he saw together, he says; Jeremy who he saw with you next day, a peddler in red stockings, and a man lightly scarred by smallpox."

"Who would that be, I wonder?"

"Aye, who? That's what we'd all like to know. Especially me, for he's the one, mark my words, that's got my cloth. But some folk, you see, Tom, think he doesn't exist at all, just something Mr. Defoe made up out of whole cloth, as we say. Mr. Defoe has been in prison, you know, Tom, and even in the pillory, for writing pamphlets against the government.

Of course that's a long time past now, but you can understand how folk feel. But see, Tom, there's a letter come for you from Mr. Defoe. I've brought it down for you, that's why I've come; here it is, come all the way from London. It's an honor for you, lad—happen," he added doubtfully.

It was indeed an honor, I thought, taking the double-folded paper in my hand, for a poorhouse boy accused of theft to receive a letter from the great Mr. Defoe. I own I found difficulty in reading it, for though the hand was clear and bold, I had never read writing sloping in that way before—indeed I had never seen a handwritten letter before at all. However, I went at it slowly and carefully, and by degrees made it out. It was addressed to Master Thomas Leigh, at the house of Mr. Stephen Firth, Upper High Royd, Barseland, Halifax, Yorkshire. I broke the seal, my fingers trembling with excitement. When I had gone through it twice, I offered it to Mr. Firth.

"Read it to me, Tom," said he.

I read it aloud, thus:

Master Thomas Leigh.

Dear Tom,

I have received from Sir Henry Norton, an estimable magistrate of the Halifax neighborhood, an account of your statement of the stealing of the cloth from your master's tenters, witnessed by you, and your courageous attempt to halt the thieves in their nefarious purpose. I have sent to Sir Henry a sworn deposition, to wit that I saw a peddler with scarlet stockings in close conversation with the man whom you next day introduced to me as Jeremy Oldfield and another man whose face appeared to be pocked as with smallpox, on a certain night in the Rose and Crown Inn, Halifax. Their discourse together appeared to me not altogether friendly, but presently they seemed to reach an agreement and money passed between them, the pockmarked man being the donor and the other the recipients.

As I remember with gratitude your excellent description of the conduct of the textile trade, which is of assistance to me in preparing my forthcoming TOUR THROUGH ENGLAND AND WALES, *and as I have had much experience of Courts and Trials, I take it upon me to offer some advice. First, urge your master and the Constable of Barseland to make every effort to discover the stolen cloth, for if this can be found and traced to the thieves, their guilt will be established beyond all doubt. Secondly, write down carefully in advance of the trial the statement which you wish to make to the Court, and arrange all its particulars in good order, so that one leads on rationally to the next. To give evidence in a Court of Assize before a Judge is an experience which may try the boldest spirit, and though I have every confidence in your courage, my dear Tom, you are young in years and may be caused much uneasiness by the examining Counsel.*

> *Your true friend,*
> *Daniel Defoe*

I felt cheered and heartened as I read. But Mr. Firth seemed not so deeply impressed.

"Where does it get us after all, Tom?" said he.

"You do not believe me, Mr. Firth," said I with great bitterness.

"Why, I *want* to believe you, Tom," said he, hesitating. "As for that accursed Jeremy, I wish he had never crossed my doorstep. Though he's a good weaver. But Mrs. Firth, you see—" He broke off, then gave a smile. "There is one at Upper High Royd who believes in you. Gracie has been baking for you, though I told her you would not be able to eat her wares."

He gestured with his hand to the table at my bedside, where a small round golden cake, with plums in, stood on a plate. Something in its size and color reminded me of little Gracie, and being weak as I was, I found tears in my eyes.

"Thank her from me with all my heart," I said, speaking as strongly as I could. "I shall try to deserve her trust. I shall eat the cake tomorrow. Was Sandy hurt? I fear Jeremy threw him very roughly aside."

"Not a whit," said Mr. Firth in a more cheerful tone. "He was fretful about a hind paw for a day or two, but has forgotten it now. Cats, Tom, have very supple bodies." He rose and made to leave me. "As for believing in you, Tom," he said, hesitating at the door, "I should not bring a cake from Gracie to you, lad, if I—on the other hand—"

"Mrs. Firth was vexed," said I.

He gave a kind of snort and went out.

I lay for a long time in misery, for I saw well enough how I was distrusted—Jeremy was a West Riding man, and though the peddler was a Londoner, they were used to his bland way of speech; I was a stranger and a poorhouse brat. I had thought I had acted well at the tenters and might even be commended, so to find myself a suspected thief was almost more than I could bear. As the dusk descended my spirit grew dark too.

Then suddenly Harry came bouncing in, with Robert carrying lights.

"Helloa, Tom! I hear you have come to your senses," he cried cheerfully. "I am heartily glad of it. Why, here is a cake asking to be eaten," he cried, stretching out his hand toward the dish.

"It is a gift to me from Mr. Firth's little girl," said I in a hurry.

Harry, hearing the feeling in my tone, at once with true courtesy drew back his hand from the cake and changed the subject.

"You are quite yourself, Tom. Hear me my lessons," he

urged—knowing, I expect, that he complimented me by this. "Robert, fetch the pile of books from my chamber." He threw himself down at the foot of my bed, and when the man had gone out said quickly: "You are sad, Tom. I hear Mr. Firth has been to see you. Courage, man! You have done no wrong. Right will triumph. The cloth will be found and traced to that pair of scoundrels."

"I wish I knew where to look," said I.

"You must think. It's useless for me to think on the matter for I know nothing of cloth. Thanks, Robert; put them on the bed."

"I cannot hear your Latin, Harry, for I know none."

"Let it be geography, then," said Harry. "Take this atlas, see, and hear me the rivers, capes and principal towns of Yorkshire."

I had never held an atlas, or seen maps close at hand before this, so I was somewhat perplexed. Harry leaned over to show me the big map of Yorkshire—each county spreading over two pages—and he pointed out to me Halifax, and the tiny circle of Barseland, and several other towns, with rivers winding, and little rows of peaked mountains. He was thus asprawl when Sir Henry came in upon us, and Sir Henry was not pleased. He told Harry rather sharply that it was dinnertime and he must come downstairs; Harry began to collect his books.

"Sir Henry," I said, sitting up and speaking respectfully: "I wish I could go to see Mr. Gledhill tomorrow morning."

"Why?" said Sir Henry in his sharp tone.

"I have something to tell him."

"Why not tell it to me?"

"Mr. Gledhill knows all about cloth, Father," said Harry.

Sir Henry frowned. "Well, that is true," he said. "Robert shall take you. If you have anything to say which may clear up this matter of the stolen cloth, you may tell it to Mr. Gledhill, seeing he is the Constable of Barseland."

"I saw Jeremy and the peddler tearing off the cloth," said I firmly.

Sir Henry compressed his lips and went away, his hand on Harry's shoulder. I heard Robert lock the door behind them, and first I grieved and then I raged, and then I grew coldly calm and planned what I should say to Mr. Gledhill. For a thought had come to me from Harry's maps, and if it should prove correct, then the whole mystery was solved.

I was still very weak next day, and had to cling to Robert's arm, but we reached Mr. Gledhill's house at last after resting by the roadside. The house, High Royd by name, was larger than Mr. Firth's, with three gables and rounded stones topping the gateposts and a very big barn. And when the door was opened to us we found it very busy: three looms going upstairs, Mrs. Gledhill (I suppose) and a couple of maids baking, Mr. Gledhill sitting at his accounts, and several men and lads moving about on textile errands. Mr. Gledhill came to us somewhat flushed; his usual quiet serious look was in abeyance.

"Well, Tom Leigh?" he said. "Sir Henry's set you loose, has he? Not before time."

"No, sir. I wish to speak to you in private."

Mr. Gledhill looked around; every corner seemed filled. "Come out to the barn," he said.

"I've been bidden not to let t'lad out o' my sight, sir," said Robert.

"Come and stand at the barn door, then, where you can see and not hear," said Mr. Gledhill, rather more quickly and roughly than was his custom.

He led me out to the barn, and there beside the two smart brown horses, and the sacks of oats, and the harness, he turned up a couple of wooden boxes and we sat down.

"Well, now. Don't be afraid, lad; speak your mind."

"Thank you for being so kind to me, Mr. Gledhill," I said.

"You've been shabbily treated, Tom," burst out Mr. Gledhill. There was no doubt as to his feeling; he was deeply angered. "You should have been given a reward, not locked up as a thief. Stephen Firth makes to be a good warm-hearted man; he should have stood up for you. I make nothing of his missus, but what can you expect from that old tyrant Sykes's daughter? My wife's her cousin, you know. Meg was visiting us when she fell in with Stephen; he's rued it often, I'll bet a pack of wool. But all the same Stephen has some sense; he should have seen through yon Jeremy long ago. You needn't tell me about the stone on your elbow, and the way he left you hanging on the hook, and the cat, and all that."

"How do you know about his persecutions of me?" said I, astonished.

"From little Gracie Firth, when Stephen left her here for the night. Lord, how that child talked! She was fearfully distressed that you should be left alone in the house with Jeremy—seemed to think he'd murder you. Well, it wasn't so far off that, either, come to think. She almost had me walking up to Upper High Royd to see if you were safe."

"Oh, how I wish you had come!" said I with a heartfelt sigh.

"Aye, but then we should not have caught the thieves," said Mr. Gledhill shrewdly. "Howsomever, this is unprofitable talk and simply vexes me further. That liverish Swain is against you, and Sir Henry of course must be impartial. Besides, he lives by his rents; he knows nowt of cloth. Now, have you aught fresh to tell me?"

"Mr. Gledhill, you know the cloth trade."

"I don't say otherwise."

"Then you will know how difficult it would be for a thief to carry a stolen piece of cloth from Barseland to Halifax without discovery, and to sell it anywhere in the West Riding. Jeremy and the peddler would be recognized at once carrying a piece of cloth over their shoulder near Barseland if it were daytime, and men do not carry pieces to Halifax or other market towns except on market days. On other days they would be observed as strange."

"The cloth could be carried in the peddler's pack."

"But the peddler did not leave Barseland that night, has not left it since the theft. Nor Jeremy either. Nor myself," I added bitterly.

"We know all this, Tom—even Swain admits all this. The cloth must have been hidden somewhere not far from the Fleece Inn."

"Indoors, then," said I. "A great heap—eighteen yards— of blue, in this brown October landscape would stick out like a sore thumb."

"Covered with leaves, perhaps," said Mr. Gledhill thoughtfully. "But we have searched closely—everyone in Barseland has searched, and we have found nothing."

"Some third person, some accomplice of Jeremy and the peddler's, must have taken the cloth away."

"We have thought of this long ago, Tom. Swain thought at first, of the earlier thefts, that it was your father."

"What?" I cried aghast. "My father? The best, the most honorable of men!"

"He was a stranger, Tom."

"There had been thefts before we came."

"Swain thought you had been in the neighborhood before the night of your father's death. But the letters from Lavenham disproved this."

"I shall never forgive Mr. Swain! How dare he! Jeremy

and the peddler murdered my father!" I cried hotly, and I poured out all the story of the night in Mearclough, and the peddler's cry of *Keep to the left* which had sent father to his death.

"The peddler speaks in a squeaking sort of tone," said Mr. Gledhill.

"He affects it. If you had heard him on the night he stole Mr. Firth's cloth! He roared like a lion."

"Well, we are no nearer the cloth, Tom."

"The accomplice took the cloth away in a cart."

"A cart? Happen. But whose cart? There is many a cart round Barseland. And how could he sell the cloth? Not in any Cloth Hall; to gain entry to Cloth Halls there are names to give and dues to pay. In the West Riding, to sell outside the Cloth Halls is against the law; I do not say it is never done, but at present the talk of Stephen Firth's stolen blue cloth is all over the West Riding; none would dare to buy or harbor it."

"All over the *West* Riding," said I.

"That's what I said. That's why Swain suspected your father—a stranger who could take the cloth elsewhere and sell it without comment."

"The peddler sells mittens which come from the *North* Riding, from a long way north, in Dent."

Mr. Gledhill gave me a quick look.

"Somebody takes the cloth in a cart toward the north, where they do not make cloth and there are no Cloth Halls and cloth can be sold openly," I said, "and perhaps brings back mittens and other things for the peddler to sell."

"Well—go on," said Mr. Gledhill. "Who is this unknown person?"

"Mittens—and mutton," said I, hesitating.

"Speak out, lad!" cried Mr. Gledhill impatiently.

"Mr. Hollas of the poorhouse drives to Skipton to buy

mutton from his cousin," I said. "And from Harry's map I see that Skipton is on the way toward Dent."

Mr. Gledhill stared at me.

"The night before I was apprenticed Mr. Swain's tenters were robbed. Next morning Mr. Hollas was not at the poorhouse. It will be easy, surely, to find whether Mr. Hollas set off for Skipton the day after Mr. Firth's tenters were robbed."

"If he is guilty, he will deny it and confuse the dates."

"If you went to Skipton immediately, without telling Mr. Hollas, and found his cousin," I pleaded.

"He will have sold the cloth long before now."

"Someone may remember it—the piece was a bright blue, like the one before."

"We have no pattern."

"I know who might be able to give you a pattern!" I cried. "The merchant who bought the previous piece. Don't you remember, Mr. Gledhill? He matched a pattern to the piece and bought it from Jeremy as he stood at your side in the Cloth Hall."

"You are a sharp lad, Tom," said Mr. Gledhill. "It was Mr. Rowlands, a very noted merchant who deals much with foreign parts. He may still have the cloth or the pattern."

"Take me with you to Skipton," I begged, "to find the peddler's other accomplice."

Mr. Gledhill gazed at me.

"Other accomplice," he repeated slowly.

"Mr. Defoe said he saw Jeremy and the peddler with a third man."

"I have not seen the deposition yet; it came only yesterday."

"But my letter says so. Look! I have a letter from Mr. Defoe," I said proudly, drawing it out from my pocket. (My scissors were no longer there; Sir Henry had impounded them.)

Mr. Gledhill read the letter very carefully. At one point he started, or so it seemed to me; but I could not quite make out what word had pricked him. When he had finished he sat for a long moment with the letter in his hand. Then he spoke, quite in his former slow, mild way.

"Tom, you must not say a word of this to anyone. Not to Harry, not to Mr. Firth, not to Gracie, not to Robert. I will come to see Sir Henry this afternoon. Do not be troubled further, lad; we shall clear you and your father too."

So it came about that a few days later Mr. Gledhill and I set off to go to Skipton. We went by public coach from Halifax one morning. I was astonished to see a knot of people gathered round as we came out of the inn: Mr. Firth was there with his mouth pulled down and tears in his eyes, quite pale and wretched, and Gracie at his side sobbed openly. As I put my foot on the step she rushed forward and wrapped her arms round my neck. Her cheek was wet against mine, and her tears ran down inside my neckcloth. I felt most awkward and reluctant under her embrace, at first, but then I grew sorry for the child's grief, and put my arms about her and hugged her and kissed her cheek, and said: "Now, Gracie love, now," in a soothing tone.

"I don't want you to go away, Tom," sobbed Gracie.

"I shall soon be back, love," said I cheerfully.

(This way of saying *love* is a Yorkshire custom, and I used it on purpose to cheer her.)

"You are good and have done nothing wrong and I love you," wailed Gracie.

At this the crowd laughed, though not unkindly, and I could not but smile a little, while the hot color came in my cheeks, but then I was vexed that anybody should presume to laugh at so sweet and warmhearted a child, who had always defended me, and I said firmly:

"I love you too, Gracie."

There was something in my tone which, I was glad to see, stopped the crowd's titters, and they looked at us with sympathy until Mr. Firth stepped forward and lifted her out of my arms.

"I don't want you to go to prison, Tom," wailed Gracie.

This startled me, and I turned swiftly on Mr. Gledhill.

"Get in and be silent," he said.

He put his hand on my shoulder and pushed me into the coach. The other passengers gazed at me with interest and would perhaps have spoken to me, but Mr. Gledhill put his finger on his lips in a solemn fashion.

In a few miles the coach drew up at a lane end, and Mr. Gledhill and I dismounted. I waited till the coach had driven off, and then I turned on him.

"I think I have a right to know what this mention of prison means," I said.

"That's right, Tom. Barseland and Halifax believe I am taking you to York Castle to prison."

"And is this true?" I gasped.

"Nay, lad, you know me better than that. We are going to Skipton, but Hollas must not guess our destination, so we take a long way round. Here, prompt to the word, comes the coach for us."

At first I was too much upset by the sudden alarm and its relief to take much notice of the landscape through which we passed, but presently I began to enjoy the many hills which, as we drew nearer Skipton, seemed higher and of a lighter rock than those near Barseland, while the valleys seemed wider and less tumultuously arranged. The number of hills in the country of Yorkshire will always continue to astonish me.

It was evening light when we reached Skipton. I took a fancy to this town, for it was more like the towns of Suffolk to which I was accustomed than those of Yorkshire. A fine broad marketplace led up to an old castle and a handsome church; on the left was an old half-timbered building which we were told was the gaol, and here we met the Constable of the township. By this time I was so sleepy I could hardly hold myself upright, so I have no recollection at all of this gentleman, save that he seemed to demur to my presence. But Mr. Gledhill insisted, and accordingly I trailed after them till we stopped in front of a neat house, not over large but a merchant's house, and well kept.

Mr. Gledhill shook me by the shoulder.

"Wake up, Tom!" he said. "I want you to look at this man we shall see here, John Hollas by name, a linen-draper, and tell me if you have seen him before. He may be Daniel Defoe's pockmarked man, you know."

The name of Daniel Defoe brought me awake quickly enough and I stepped forward as the Constable knocked. A neat maidservant admitted the three of us and showed us into a parlor at the back and lighted the candles and went to fetch her master. I stood all agog, waiting for the entrance of this pockmarked man and thinking how exciting it was that a letter for me from a great writer in London should have led us over hill and dale to this thief. Then Mr. John Hollas entered the room.

He was a short, plump man, very neatly dressed with bright shoe buckles and a well-curled wig; florid in complexion and completely smooth of skin.

I was so utterly cast down and confounded—for knowing Daniel Defoe to be absolutely exact in all his observations I had believed him entirely about the smallpox—that I staggered back and almost fell, then with an effort I rallied myself and forced myself to gaze earnestly again into his face. But there was not a pockmark on him.

"Well, Tom?" said Mr. Gledhill dryly under cover of the Constable's explanation of our errand. "Do you know him?"

I shook my head and shrank back. This brought me to the windows, and gazing out in a daze of misery I muttered dully:

"There is Dobbin."

"Dobbin?" exclaimed Mr. Gledhill, stepping toward me. "The horse from Barseland poorhouse."

"It is my cousin, then, and we can clear up this matter of the blue cloth at once, gentlemen," said John Hollas. "For I assure you that I do not deal in stolen goods."

He stepped toward the hearth to pull the bell, but I was so eager to be out of the way of these men who must be thinking of me as a fool and a liar that without a pause for thought I ran out and along the passage and through the kitchen and out of the back door, crying: "Mr. Hollas! Mr. Hollas!"

Mr. Hollas of the Barseland poorhouse was just dismounting from the cart, so that he had his back to me, but he heard my cry and turned to me with a smile. I gaped and halted, amazed, for in the light and shadow between the parlor candles and the setting sun, his freckles made dark spots on his cheeks, so that his face looked pitted.

I gave a loud cry and bounded toward him, and his face changed to fury, and he flung himself up into the driver's seat and whipped up the horse, and the cart clattered off down the narrow back street, swaying from side to side. I flew after him, and as I pounded down the street I suddenly remembered my great-grandfather and how he earned the silver watch, and my heart rose hot and strong within me, and I thought: I can do what my great-grand-father did, I can catch the horse!

And I doubled my speed and hurled myself down the street, and the people standing there screamed and ran aside, and I drew level with the cart wheel and I saw it bump and turn and slide, and then there was Dobbin's heaving brown flank and the long cart shaft, and a sharp pain across my neck and shoulders where Hollas had struck me with the whiplash, and then I caught one rein and pulled at it, and Dobbin slewed round toward me, and everything was huge yellow horse's teeth and wide nostrils and mane flopping and great rolling eyes and trampling hoofs, and in the background Hollas standing up, lashing wildly at me, and I thought Dobbin was going to swing me off my feet but I caught the other rein by his mouth and pulled down as hard as I could, and suddenly everything was still.

Dobbin stood quiet, trembling, the cart had swung across the street and hit the wall of a house and was jammed there, passers-by had pulled Hollas off the cart and held his arms behind his back, and Mr. Gledhill stood beside me with his hand on my shoulder, saying:

"Well done, Tom."

And so I am sitting comfortably in the housebody at Upper High Royd, writing down, with pens sharpened by Gracie, all that has happened to me since I came to Yorkshire. I have done no carding nor weaving for many days. But I hope soon to be back at work, for tomorrow we go to York, and the day after (I think) we shall be at the York assizes, and I shall be giving evidence before the Court.

The evidence is very strong now against Jeremy and the peddler. Mr. John Hollas of Skipton, an honest man who had no notion that the goods he bought from his cousin were stolen, admitted frankly that he had bought from poorhouse Hollas, and sold in the Monday market at Skipton, a length of blue cloth which matched the pattern Mr. Gledhill had obtained from the merchant Rowlands to show him. The cloth had been sold to a Skipton tailor, who had made it up for a country gentleman, his customer. All these people were traced and gave their depositions, and Mr. John Hollas was so angry with his cousin for having involved him in dishonesty that he took his oath that he had bought the cloth openly and honestly from him. At this George Hollas (of the freckles and the poorhouse) said he had bought the cloth honestly from the peddler. But nobody believed him, for one does not buy honestly in the middle of the night, as he must have done; and if he were guiltless, why did he run from me? It is rumored, therefore, that he will turn King's Evidence, and go into the witness box against Jeremy and the peddler.

Sir Henry Norton and Harry, Mr. Gledhill, Mr. Swain, Mr. and Mrs. Firth and Gracie and myself of course, are all going to York by coach tomorrow, and it is thought in Barseland that Mr. Sykes may go to the assizes also, to prove malice aforethought by the peddler, because of the false message about his health. There is a good deal of joking about Mr. Sykes in Barseland, and Harry tells me he has heard his father say he hopes the old fool will not go, for he will be sure to make a mess of the case. Mrs. Firth has had my suit washed and brushed and has made me a new neckcloth, and I am to wear white stockings, and my hair tied back in a black bow. I own I am excited by the prospect of the trial, and if all goes well I intend to write down an account of it on my return.

I HAD BEEN so much instructed and exhorted about the trial
—by Mr. Firth, Mr. Gledhill and even by Sir Henry—that I
felt I knew all about it beforehand, but this did not prove to
be the case. Indeed one of the things I have learned in the
past year, which has turned me from a thoughtless boy into a
responsible lad, is that the unexpected is always awaiting one
round the corner; one must accustom oneself to face these
surprising occurrences without flinching, if one is to be at all
satisfied with one's own behavior. We had not been in York
an hour before a very great surprise fell upon me.

It happened in this way. There was a great to-do and
bustle at the inn, settling into the various chambers which
had been engaged for us, with myself running up and down
with our baggage—a small bandbox of Mrs. Firth's had been
misplaced and I had much ado to find it. Then all our party
seemed to vanish behind their doors, to wash and change
after the journey, I suppose, because when I knocked at
Mr. and Mrs. Firth's door to ask permission to go out for a
while, Mr. Firth was in his shirt sleeves and without a wig.

"Yes, yes," he said hastily. "Be off with you. But don't be
too long, Tom," he called after me as I went down the
stairs.

I was walking toward the huge cathedral which I could
see in the distance—it is called the Minster, and has three
great towers—but progressing slowly because of the crowded
pavements and narrow streets, when suddenly ahead of me
by the bank of the river I saw the manufacturer who had

hired my father to leave Lavenham and come to the West Riding! At first I could not believe my eyes; I stared and gasped; but yes, it was most certainly he; the short stout body, in the cinnamon cloth suit, the head held so far back that he seemed to look down his nose at his own paunch, the round, florid face, the turned-out toes, the air of self-importance—it was he! I shouted and remembered I did not know what name to shout, and tried to hurl myself toward him, but he strutted along ahead of me and entered the archway of one of the great gates of the old York walls. By the time I reached this archway he had disappeared.

Then I thought: I shall be able to see which way he has gone if I look down at the streets from above; and I ran up the steps and onto the walls; and I could not see him amid the throng and so I ran a few steps farther, and so it came about that I found myself quite a long way from the archway I knew, and alone on the walls. Then I came to a flight of steps leading downward and stupidly thought it would be quicker and more direct to return on the ground, and so descended. In a word, I well and truly lost myself, and it was a clock hour before I found myself again at the doorway of my inn.

I stepped in quickly and found myself the center of a circle of accusing eyes: our whole party was drawn up in a ring gazing angrily at me—our whole party, with one addition: the gentleman with the back-held head and the turned-out toes.

"Where have you been, Tom?" said Mr. Firth, very much vexed.

"I lost myself chasing that gentleman," said I, pointing to the cinnamon suit.

"Chasing *me?*" said he in a prim tone, elevating his nose.

"You are the one who hired my father, sir, in Lavenham," I panted.

"What, what?"

"You hired my father, in Lavenham, to come and weave for you in the West Riding."

"Why, it is true I engaged a weaver, but he did not come."

"Do you not remember me, sir? I ran into the cottage and tripped over your foot."

"That was a much smaller boy, a dirty little child. Who is this great lad?"

"This is Thomas Leigh, my apprentice," said Mr. Firth. "He accompanied his father, and came on Barseland poorhouse when his father was drowned in the beck."

"What was his father doing in Barseland?"

"He had lost his way, no doubt. But why did you appoint him to meet you at Halifax market?" said Mr. Firth. He spoke grimly, as if this was the last straw on an irritation which had been piling for a long time. "Huddersfield is your nearest town, Mr. Sykes."

"Mr. Sykes!" I exclaimed.

"Aye, it is Mr. Sykes," said Mr. Firth as before.

Mr. Sykes's fair face flushed. "I do not want all my fellow manufacturers to know my business," he said in his pompous tones. "I am one who, as you know, Stephen, prefers to keep his affairs to himself. It would be better for you if you did the same."

"What!" exclaimed Mr. Firth angrily. "To what affairs do you refer, sir?"

"Stephen! Father!" moaned Mrs. Firth.

"Well, no matter," said Mr. Sykes in his stately way. "No matter, Stephen."

"It was your being ill which dragged me from Upper High Royd and left my tenters open to theft, let me remind you, Mr. Sykes."

"I was not ill and sent no message."

"Gentlemen, gentlemen, we must go to Sergeant Braithwaite," said Sir Henry. "We are late already, and Sergeant Braithwaite is not a man whom one can delay with impunity."

"All this time I have fed and housed the boy, while he should have been at your charges."

"I deny that. In any case, how could I know aught of the boy? You told me nothing. I have not seen my daughter for six months."

"You did not invite us," snapped Mr. Firth.

"You wrote me no letter about the boy."

"Why should I? I did not know you had any connection with him."

"Gentlemen, I must insist that you accompany me at once," said Sir Henry in a stern magisterial tone.

So we set off, and went to call upon Mr. Sergeant Braithwaite, who was to be one of the Counsel for the Prosecution in the trial; for it seems this word *sergeant*, which I had always thought of only in a military way, was applied also to high officers of the law.

Of this visit I remember almost nothing. I am told that the sergeant took me through my whole story and deposition, but I do not recall it, for I was lost in misery. To be the occasion of a disagreement between Mr. Firth and his wife's father was a most wretched thing for me; only less wretched, indeed, than to hear my master grumble about my cost as his apprentice. The sight of Mr. Sykes, too, had recalled to my mind my dear father, and Lavenham and our journey and the Barseland beck in Mearclough, and I felt the pain of my bereavement as keenly as the moment when I first heard it. I was not surprised to hear Sergeant Braithwaite— who was a small sharp man with very bright black eyes— say in a complaining tone:

"He looks very hangdog."

"He is not used to look so; he is a lad of spirit," said Sir Henry in a reproachful tone.

"Does your arm yet pain you?" inquired the sergeant. "I see it is still in a sash."

"Not much," said I, drearily and not quite truthfully. "If you wish me to take off the sash—"

"No, no! You must keep it bound till after the trial," said the sergeant hastily. "What is wrong with you, then, Tom Leigh?"

"I am just—grieved," said I, turning my head aside.

"Nay, don't grieve, Tom," said Mr. Firth more kindly. "It is not your fault. But I cannot help but feel vexed."

Mrs. Firth, who was sitting with her mouth primmed up and her head turned aside, gave a small sob.

"Come, come, good people!" exclaimed Mr. Braithwaite, smiling—he was hard put to it not to laugh outright at us, it seemed to me. "We are to prosecute thieves tomorrow, remember. These megrims will not suit our judge, Sir Gervase King, I promise you. You will need all your wits at hand."

And so indeed it proved. We were all still somewhat sullen when we set off to the court in the morning, but when we had reached the huge York Castle, passed through the heavy archway with its round towers, made our way up the long curving drive and climbed the flight of steps, all thronged with people, attorneys in gowns bustling about and ordinary folk in their best clothes, looking perplexed and miserable if they were witnesses, grinning and curious if they were spectators—then we began to feel overawed and thankful to have Barseland people near us. We were put into a small place for witnesses with a court officer and the door shut on us, and were summoned into court one by one. Mr. Firth went first, looking pale. Mrs. Firth wept at his departure, and her father rebuked her in his prim tones.

"Your grief is excessive, my dear Margaret; pray control yourself," said he.

Mr. Gledhill was next; I gathered from the talk that Mr. Firth had to witness that the cloth was on the tenters when he left Upper High Royd at five in the afternoon, and Mr. Gledhill to prove that it was not there at ten o'clock that night.

Presently Mr. Sykes's name was called, and he walked out with his usual stately, pigeon-toed step, and his head held stiff. A few minutes later we thought we heard a gale of laughter coming from the court; Sir Henry and Mr. Swain exchanged meaning glances, and Harry winked at me, but from respect to Mrs. Firth nobody made any remark.

Then at last my name came echoing down the passage: "Call Thomas Leigh! Call Thomas Leigh!"

I rose and made for the door, feeling as if my stomach would drop out.

"Good luck, Tom!" said Harry soberly.

"Aye, good luck!" they all cried.

"Speak the truth and you have nothing to fear," added Sir Henry.

To me this sounded like one of those conventional pious exhortations grown folk think it right to give to youngsters, which are not always easy to believe. However, I did my best with this from Sir Henry, since it was the only support I was likely to receive.

The officer opened the door and ushered me into the court and another led me to the witness box.

A waft of hot air struck me in the face, for the large lofty chamber was crowded, faces ranked in tiers reaching up to the roof. The first thing which drew my eye was on a table to one side: a blue piece of ours, and a well-cut suit of breeches, coat and waistcoat of the same blue, beside it. I remembered now having heard Sergeant Braithwaite say the day before that the piece was the one bought by Mr. Rowlands, fetched back from Holland for the case, and the suit the one tailored in Skipton from the stolen piece. The blue stood out bright and I felt proud of it.

Aloft on a dais, before a great colored, embossed royal coat of arms, sat the judge in a flowing red gown with ermine somewhere at his shoulders, and one look put me in awe of him. He had a very handsome, lean, beaked face, with the most piercing, gleaming gray eyes I have ever seen—they were like points of steel. He sat very easily in his great carved chair, but perfectly still. His hands rested on some papers on the table before him, very fine, long and white and delicate. His voice, when he spoke, was silvery but strong, like steel again, easy to hear; every word was very clearly and beautifully said but with no affectation. He looked at me and I felt pierced to the marrow.

"How old is this witness, Sergeant Braithwaite?" said the judge.

"Fourteen, my lord."

Sergeant Braithwaite, whom I now looked at, appeared much more dignified and imposing, now that he was in his gown, than he had done yesterday.

"Do you intend that he shall take the oath, being as he is a minor?"

"That is as your lordship pleases. I think he is competent."

"Thomas Leigh, do you understand the meaning of an oath?"

"Yes, my lord," I whispered from a dry throat.

"Speak up. Do you understand what it means to tell the truth, the whole truth, and nothing but the truth?"

If I had not understood it before, I understood the words when he spoke them. I felt ashamed to be giving evidence on my master's behalf in this timid, blundering way before a judge I admired so much; I gathered my strength together and clenched my hands and said: "Yes, my lord," firmly.

"Give him the oath."

A clerk of the court came up to me and made me repeat after him the words of the oath to tell the truth. When this was over he stepped away and sat down; my eyes followed him and suddenly I saw Jeremy and the peddler and Mr. Hollas in the dock. Jeremy was filthy, in rags, unshaven, his hair tousled, and so downcast and bowed that I felt almost sorry for him; Mr. Hollas looked a pale quivering little worm, his freckles very dark across his face. But the peddler looked neat and jaunty, well shaven, with a clean shirt and neckcloth, though without his coat; he held his head up and glanced about him cheerfully, caught my eye and nodded to me! I turned away in horror.

Sergeant Braithwaite began to ask me my name and address and occupation. Looking back on it now, I find my giving of evidence fell into three periods: at first I was so terrified I had great difficulty in finding my words and my voice, and was so afraid of making a mistake that I stumbled and hesitated; then the great interest of the matter I had to tell, and my indignation over it, overpowered my fear and I spoke fast and boldly; then toward the end I grew so tired from the searching questions of both judge and counsel that I could hardly hold up my head, and I spoke with difficulty, slowly. What remains with me most strongly is the acuteness of the counsel and even more of the judge; these were men far more clever than any I had met before. It was not just that they were skilled in the law; they saw to the heart of the matter, the essential point of what I said, and if I let slip any word which was not entirely accurate, they pounced on it and wrestled with it until my meaning was plain.

"Where were you born? And you lived there till when?

You came with your father to the West Riding for what purpose? Do you see in the court the manufacturer who hired your father?"

Sergeant Braithwaite was looking at the jury as he asked this question; naturally my glance followed his, and I was somewhat disconcerted not to see Mr. Sykes. However, I looked all round and discovered him sitting next to Mr. Firth. My master sat erect and looked more composed and master of himself than I had ever seen him, whereas Mr. Sykes's fair face was flushed and he appeared somewhat deflated—like one of those pig's bladders which can be blown up, and squeak and wrinkle as the air is let out. As I pointed him out and named him the spectators gave a titter, Mr. Sykes flushed even deeper and the judge gave a slight acid smile—I guessed, rightly as it proved, that Mr. Sykes had shown his pompous conceit and silliness in the witness box and been well taken down for it.

Mr. Braithwaite now, to my surprise, led me on to tell of our terrible first night in Barseland, and how my father and I made our way down beside the stream in Mearclough.

"And what caused your father to fall down the steep bank of this stream?"

"A voice which cried out loudly: *Keep to the left!* The stream bent sharply to the right at this point, so that by obeying the voice's instruction my father plunged straight down the bank—to his death."

"One moment, Mr. Braithwaite," intervened the judge at this point.

"My lord?"

"To what indictment are you pleading, sergeant? This in front of me," said the judge smoothly, tapping the paper with his long white forefinger, "speaks of *cutting and stealing cloth from the tenters of Stephen Firth of Upper High*

Royd and unlawfully selling the same. I understood you were to plead to that indictment?"

"I am pleading to that indictment, my lord."

"But what has all this about streams at midnight to do with cutting and stealing from tenters?"

"My lord, it is the defendants' contention that Thomas Leigh, by reason of a suspicion he entertained that the defendants were concerned in his father's death, brought this accusation falsely against them for prejudice."

"And what is your intention in this matter?"

"To show that Thomas Leigh did not, in fact, suspect the defendants of being concerned in his father's death, until after the commission of the theft, my lord."

"You take a very odd road to it, Mr. Braithwaite. However, pray go on."

"Your father's neck was broken by his fall?" resumed the sergeant.

"He was dead when I reached him," said I in a voice which shook.

"And what happened then?"

"I bent over him and tried to drag him from the water, and something struck me on the head and I knew no more."

"Witness," said the judge, leaning forward: "Tell me: did you recognize the voice which called out to your father?"

"Not at the time, my lord."

"Had you heard the voice before that occasion?"

I was about to say *Never*, when it struck me that either the peddler or Jeremy or both must have been in the Fleece Inn when my father showed his gold and took his directions. I therefore hesitated, and answered carefully:

"Not to my knowledge then, my lord."

The judge nodded and sat back.

The sergeant now questioned me about the poorhouse,

Mr. Hollas' absences and returns, and my apprenticeship to Mr. Firth.

"Shall we come to the tenters in an hour or so, Mr. Braithwaite?" inquired the judge.

He did not seem to resent the laughter which followed, though officers of the court shouted: "Silence!" very loudly.

"At once, my lord," said the sergeant, bowing. He turned to me. "Had you any suspicion during the period you worked together, that Jeremy Oldfield intended to steal from your master?"

This perplexed me; I hesitated, and the crowd began to whisper.

"Not at the time," I said at length.

"What do you mean by that?" put in the judge sharply.

"Jeremy showed himself an enemy to me," I said, "in many ways." (I named them.) "I could not at the time understand why. But later I saw that his intention was to get rid of me, so as to leave Upper High Royd empty for the theft."

"Later? When was that?"

"On the night of the theft."

"If we could come to the night of the theft, Mr. Braithwaite," said the judge in his smooth biting tones, "it would, I believe, be of assistance to the witness as well as to the court."

"As your lordship pleases," said the sergeant, bowing again. "It is necessary to substantiate first when the stolen piece was put on the tenters. This witness can provide corroborative evidence."

"Very well, very well," said the judge impatiently.

"The piece went to the fulling mill on Wednesday morning," said I, "and Mr. Firth fetched it back on Wednesday afternoon; then Josiah, Mr. Firth's other weaver, and I put it out on the tenters."

"Where it would remain until?"

"Until it was dry. Friday morning most probably."

"One moment—allow me, Mr. Braithwaite—I hope I do not disturb your argument," said the judge in a very polite manner. "There is one question I wish to ask the witness. This process of weaving and fulling and tentering and drying —is it possible to foretell its stages with any degree of accuracy?"

"Yes, my lord—except for the weather," said I. (At this everyone laughed.)

"Jeremy Oldfield would know when the piece was likely to be on the tenters?"

"Yes, my lord."

"How long before its completion could he know?"

"Several days, my lord, for Jeremy wove the piece himself, so he could weave fast or slow to finish it when he chose. Within reasonable limits," I added.

"Proceed, Mr. Braithwaite," said the judge. "No—one moment. I understood from the first witness, Stephen Firth, that this piece of cloth in court is of the same length and weight as the stolen piece from which the suit is made? Is that correct?"

"Yes, my lord. They are both approximately eighteen yards long, and twenty pounds in weight, as is usual for such—kerseys, I believe they are called. The two pieces were also woven from the same yarn, dyed at the same time," said the sergeant, reading these unfamiliar terms from his brief, carefully.

"I should like to see the witness handle the cloth. Mr. Firth, would you be so very kind as to carry the piece to the witness box?"

Mr. Firth, surprised but not displeased, stepped out to the table and swung the piece over his left shoulder. Left arm

akimbo, he carried it over and laid it neatly—for he was a true clothier—across the box in front of me.

"Now, Thomas Leigh, return it to the table," said the judge.

I attempted this with some apprehension, for I had in fact never shouldered a piece as yet, not being come to my full strength. But as it turned out I could not even lift it to my shoulder, having only one hand to use. I struggled to get my right arm around it and managed to do so, then as I tried to pull it upward it escaped my grasp and rolled undone to the floor.

"Come, come," said the judge severely.

I came out of the box, knelt and folded the cloth again and strove again to raise it, but in vain. Panting and hot, I scrambled to my feet and stood there looking foolish, and began to apologize and explain about my arm, but the judge interrupted me.

"Let it lie there. Return to the witness box. Proceed, Mr. Braithwaite," he said sternly.

I tried to fold the cloth to a more seemly cuttle as Yorkshire clothiers call folds, but the sergeant waved me angrily away. I felt unhappy to leave the piece thus, tumbled on the ground and gazed pleadingly at Mr. Firth for forgiveness, but he avoided my eye.

And now the sergeant began his questions again. He took me back to the first days of my apprenticeship. When had I first seen the peddler? Had I seen Jeremy have any communication with him? (Here I hesitated, and mentioned the arm-waving Jeremy had indulged in on my first day at Upper High Royd; seeing this slighted I spoke of Mr. Defoe's letter, but was told that this would be read separately later.)

And now at last we reached the day of the theft and, as I have said, I became so eager and indignant that I forgot my fears. Indeed I forgot the court, the judge, the sergeant, the crowd, the tumbled piece, and saw before my eyes only the events that I described. I spoke of the coming of the peddler with the message about Mr. Sykes, the swift departure of Mr. and Mrs. Firth and Gracie, the evening when Jeremy hurried me to bed, my discovery that I was locked in.

"How did you discover this?"

"It was the cat, sir," said I.

At this there was a great roar of laughter. The judge was furious.

"Silence!" he cried. "Silence at once! If there is any more noise of this kind, I shall clear the court. Now, Mr. Braithwaite."

"Explain about the cat, my boy," said Mr. Braithwaite in a very mild, gentle tone.

"Sandy often came to my bed to sleep with me," I said. "That night he came, and mewed as usual at my door. I went to let him in, and could not open the door. It was locked."

A hush fell on the court.

"And then?"

"I heard voices below, at the house door."

"Did you recognize these voices?"

"The speakers were Jeremy and the peddler."

"What did you do then, Thomas Leigh?"

"Everything seemed to fall into place, sir; I understood the whole plot, everything was clear."

"Never mind about that. What did you *do*?"

"I opened the taking-in doors and let myself down to the ground on the hook."

"I don't understand a word of that, Mr. Braithwaite," said the judge testily.

"Would your lordship like to excuse the witness for a moment and recall Mr. Firth on this point?"

"No. Let the boy tell it himself."

We had a long struggle—or it seemed long to me—before I managed to make clear what I had done.

"When you were on the ground, what did you do?"

"I crept round the back of the house toward the tenters— it was moonlight and the shadows were very deep and gave me cover."

"Were you not afraid to approach these two men? It was very rash," said the judge in a tone of astonishment.

"Yes, my lord," said I, coloring and hanging my head. "I was afraid. But—I was Mr. Firth's apprentice, you see." I thought of the words "good and faithful servant" in my indentures, but it seemed pretentious to utter them.

"Well—tell me what you saw, in your own words," said Mr. Braithwaite.

I told how I had seen Jeremy taking the cloth off the bottom row of nails, how the peddler stood by idle, how Jeremy had reproached him, how the peddler had thrown off his coat and knelt to work, how I had drawn the peddler's coat toward me and cut out a jagged portion of the lining.

"This is the piece of lining, my lord," said Mr. Braithwaite.

The officer of the court held it up. The spectators gasped.

"And here is the coat."

The officer of the court fitted the lining into the coat.

Then the spectators roared, and could not be silenced for some moments though the officers bellowed at them and the judge shrilled.

"Witnesses will depose—" shouted Sergeant Braithwaite, "to wit, Sir Henry Norton, justice of the peace, Mr. William Gledhill, Constable of Barseland township, and Mr. John Swain, Overseer of the poor—that this piece of lining and this coat were shown to them on the night of the theft in this condition—or rather, in the early hours of the following morning," he finished in his ordinary voice, the crowd having fallen silent from interest in what he was saying.

"Will the boy say why he cut out the piece of lining?" said the judge.

"To prove that the peddler had been there, my lord."

"How chanced it that you had scissors with you?"

"They were a gift of Mr. Firth's little daughter, Gracie, and I always carried them in my coat pocket."

Here I looked toward Mr. Firth, and saw to my surprise that Mrs. Firth and Gracie were sitting beside him. I learned afterward that before I entered the witness box Mrs. Firth had been excused from giving evidence about the peddler's message, as Mr. Firth's was deemed sufficient, so she was allowed to enter the court and Mr. Firth fetched her in.

"Why did you think to don your coat in the midst of your hurried action?" pursued the judge.

"I feared my shirt if uncovered would show very white in the moonlight."

"Well, well. Well, well, well! And why did you cut such a jagged piece, eh?"

"It was because of my indentures, my lord," said I.

It was at this point, after the long questioning and excitement of the showing of the lining, that I suddenly grew tired. I stumbled over my account of the fight with Jeremy and the breaking of my arm, and I muddled what I had heard Jeremy and the peddler say to each other at the foot of the lane. Then I made a great effort and cried out loudly when I was repeating the peddler's cry:

"Keep to the left!"

"This is the moment, my lord," said Sergeant Braithwaite, "when the witness believed he recognized the peddler's voice as the one he heard by the stream."

"Keep to the left!" cried the peddler suddenly in a high shrill almost girlish voice, and he giggled.

Everyone laughed, and the judge bade Anthony Dyce be silent without much anger in his tone.

"He did not cry out like that by the stream!" I cried angrily.

Sergeant Braithwaite shrugged, and the judge said:

"Well, we are not trying a murder case. Continue."

The sergeant took me very quickly through my climbing into Harry's window, my evidence to Sir Henry, my journey to Skipton, my stopping of Mr. Hollas' horse. Then at last my ordeal was over; I was led out of the box by a court officer, and sank down thankfully by Mr. Firth's side. He squeezed my arm gently with his hand and gave me a kind look, and I felt relieved.

I must own that I did not hear very much of the evidence which followed; I was so exhausted as to be half asleep, and —I am ashamed to say—started to wakefulness only when I heard my own name. Harry gave evidence of my climbing into his window with a broken arm and crying out that the tenters were being robbed; Sir Henry spoke of my accusation of Jeremy and the peddler and the matter of the lining; Mr. Gledhill and Mr. Swain described their arrests of the men and of the sight of the empty tenters; Mr. Defoe's deposition was read, then Mr. Gledhill was recalled to tell of our journey to Skipton. I started awake here and found everyone looking at me and felt greatly confused. Then came Mr. John Hollas, very indignant, and then a man I did not know, the Skipton tailor, I learned later. Then Mr. Sergeant Braithwaite arose and made a long speech, telling the whole story all over again; I nodded off through this, and woke presently feeling much refreshed.

"All we pray is," Mr. Braithwaite was concluding: "that the jury will give such a verdict as is agreeable to justice."

He sat down, drawing his gown sweepingly around him,

and looked expectantly at the judge. There was a slight pause, then the judge spoke.

"It is now for the accused to have their say. Anthony Dyce, what say you?"

The peddler bounced across to the witness box, bowed elaborately to the judge and began at once in a shrill cheerful tone:

"Several things have been asserted against me which are false, my lord, with respect to my intention. I had no intention whatever of stealing cloth, I never gave a message to Mrs. Firth that her father was ill, I simply said I was told in some Almondbury inn or other—"

"Which inn, Dyce?"

"The White Lion or the Fleece or the Weavers' Arms—" I could see from Mr. Sykes's swollen look that these were not the right names, and the peddler saw it too, for he added hurriedly: "I cannot remember and your lordship cannot imagine how stupidly alike all these Yorkshire inns are—I was *told* in some inn that Mr. Sykes was ill. Now I learn that Mr. Sykes often believes himself to be ill and his make-believe ailments are much talked of—but is that my fault? I simply repeated what I heard. But poor Mrs. Firth being so excessively devoted to her father"—here the peddler tittered, and all the spectators tittered with him—"went off at once into a flutter."

"This is not what Mr. Stephen Firth says, Dyce," said the judge.

"A weaver—pardon, clothier—on a remote hillside who can hardly speak the King's English is not as quick in the uptake—pardon, as swift in comprehension—as a man of intelligence and learning like yourself, my lord," said the peddler with a bow.

"Dyce, you are a saucy fellow," said the judge.

"As your lordship pleases," said the peddler with a grin.

The spectators tittered again, and my heart burned within me at the peddler's cunning.

"What have you to say on your sale of the cloth to George Hollas?"

"I have a chapman's licence, I am a licensed peddler," said the peddler on a note of grievance. "Oldfield handed me the cloth to sell, and I sold it honorably to George Hollas."

"I never!" wailed Jeremy in astonishment.

"Silence! You will have your opportunity presently, Oldfield. Now, Dyce. What do you say of Mr. Daniel Defoe's statement that he saw you with the other two accused, the week before the theft?"

"He was mistaken, my lord; I was not in Halifax at that time. After all, Mr. Daniel Defoe is a man not unacquainted with the inside of prisons; he has even stood in the pillory for a political offence. Are we to take his word against that of a decent citizen like myself?"

"Mr. Defoe's political offences are long since over," said the judge dryly. "When did Jeremy Oldfield give you the piece of cloth to sell?"

"Later that night. I understood that Tom Leigh had spoiled it for the usual market by tearing and cutting the cloth."

"So you sold it to George Hollas?"

"Just so."

"Have you anything more to say?"

"I beg your lordship to assign me counsel," said the peddler in an earnest pleading tone.

"Should any point of law arise, you shall have counsel, but as yet there is nothing but matter of fact. Have you anything more to say?"

"Nothing, my lord. I leave my case confidently in your lordship's hands," said the peddler, bowing.

"If you, Dyce, have done, then Jeremy Oldfield, what have you to say for yourself?" said the judge.

Jeremy looked utterly taken aback, as well he might after the peddler's lies.

"You have pleaded Not Guilty," said the judge impatiently. "You have heard the evidence against you. Have you anything to say in rebuttal? In your defense, I mean?"

"Aye—aye," faltered Jeremy. "Aye, I have that."

"Go into the witness box," commanded the judge. "Now, give us your account of the happenings on the night of the theft."

"It were Tom that stole t'piece," said Jeremy. "Me and peddler were sitting talking, you see—"

"What were you talking about? What was the object of Anthony Dyce's visit?"

"Oh, that. He come to—to—" stammered Jeremy. It was clear that he had forgotten the story agreed upon, and he gazed imploringly across the court at the peddler. I saw, and I think the judge saw, that the peddler slightly tapped one hand. "It were t'mittens," said Jeremy with relief. "Aye, it were t'mittens. We was sitting, you see, and we heard a noise, and we ran out, and there were Tom Leigh, pulling cloth off tenters. I yelled at him to stop, and sprang at him, and we rolled on ground."

"Have you any explanation as to how he broke his arm?"

"Nay," said Jeremy indignantly, "it weren't me as broke his arm. Nor it weren't me as talked his father down, neither—"

"Hold your tongue, you fool!" roared the peddler.

There was an awful hush in court. For the peddler had shouted as I had heard him shout, with his full man's tone. Everyone who heard him knew that, though there might not be enough evidence to convict him of being concerned in my father's death, he had incriminated himself. The judge gave a grim smile; the peddler saw what he had done, and slowly his pasty face turned a dark crimson.

"Continue, Oldfield," said the judge.

"He got away—Tom, I mean—and ran off."

"Did he carry the piece of cloth with him then?"

"Nay, it weren't right off the tenters then," said Jeremy. "Us coming out to tentercroft stopped him, d'you see."

"When do you suppose he took it away, then?"

"Why—afterward, of course."

There was a pause. Then the judge said very quietly:

"In spite of his broken arm?"

"Well—I suppose," agreed Jeremy.

"He handled the cloth as he did just now?" said the judge.

He turned his gaze slowly to the blue piece, tumbled on the floor in front of the witness box. And suddenly the spectators—and the jury too, I saw—took his point. A great roar of delight thundered from all parts of the court. Jeremy hung his head and said nothing, and I knew with an immense rush of relief that my name was cleared.

"Have you any witnesses on your behalf, Jeremy Oldfield, anyone to speak for you?" pursued the judge.

"No," muttered Jeremy.

"Have you anything more to say?"

Jeremy shook his head despondently.

"Well, George Hollas, then. What say you, Hollas?"

"Anthony Dyce is a licensed peddler, he sold me the cloth as any licensed chapman would."

"At what hour of the night did this sale occur?" inquired the judge dryly.

"It would be about midnight," said Hollas, somewhat crestfallen.

"Yet you did not doubt the honesty of the sale?"

"I had bought other goods from Anthony Dyce, and no trouble had ensued. I sometimes brought goods from Skip-

ton—mittens and such like—and we exchanged. I am confounded, my lord," went on Hollas at a great rate, as if he
had learned the words by heart, "to think that I should be
thought concerned in such a heinous crime."

"What other goods had you bought from Anthony Dyce
which caused no trouble?" inquired the judge.

Hollas hesitated. He gazed across at the peddler, who returned him a furious, forbidding look. ("This is my father's
watch," I thought.)

"Cloth," muttered Hollas at last, hanging his head.

"Have you any explanation of why you ran away from
Thomas Leigh in Skipton?"

"A young jackanapes like that comes charging down on me
and frightens my horse out of his senses, and I am blamed
for galloping off!" cried Hollas.

His tone of outraged virtue was nauseating.

There was a pause now for the candles to be lighted, then
folding his fine hands before him, the judge gave his sum-
ming up. It was the most clear, easy-to-follow, correct—and
damning—account imaginable of the whole affair; every in-
cident was in its right order, yet the actions of each person
concerned were shown in a way which revealed their meaning. The peddler's tale, and Jeremy's, and George Hollas',
were presented as proper for the jury's consideration—but on
the other hand, said the judge, and proceeded quietly to
expose each lie. Why did the peddler return late at night to
Upper High Royd? How and when was the piece of lining
cut from the peddler's coat if the peddler was innocent? Oldfield stated that Thomas Leigh had stolen the cloth, but this
conflicted with the evidence of the peddler and George Hollas, as well as with that of Thomas Leigh and with the admitted incapacity of his arm. In which of these stories did
every detail of events fit without forcing?

"I am bound to say," observed the judge presently in his

even, silvery tones, "that no point of Thomas Leigh's evidence seemed to me to be shaken, in spite of the attempts made to shake it by the accused, while the evidence of the other inhabitants of Barseland and of the piece of lining gave it strong support. It is for you to decide, members of the jury," he continued: "whether you believe this lad, cruelly orphaned and, you may think, brave, faithful and the victim of conspiracy, or prefer to confide in the contradictory and evasive testimony of the accused, two of whom seem determined to lay the blame upon the third, to his evident surprise. Honest men are not wont to make sales at midnight, and eighteen yards of heavy cloth cannot be raised to the shoulder by a boy with a broken arm. None of the accused has offered an alternative explanation of the lining cut, and proved to be cut, from the peddler's coat, and it may seem to you that this is because there is no other tenable explanation.

"If, then, upon the whole, members of the jury," he concluded, "you are satisfied from the evidence, that Jeremy Oldfield did on purpose, and of malice aforethought, unlawfully remove the cloth from Mr. Stephen Firth's tenters, and Anthony Dyce was present and assisted at this removal, and did after sell this cloth so stolen to George Hollas, and George Hollas then sold this cloth to his cousin, John Hollas of Skipton, who received it not knowing it to be stolen; if, I say, you are satisfied that this is true, then you will find Jeremy Oldfield, Anthony Dyce and George Hollas guilty. But if this has not been proved to your satisfaction, then you will find them not guilty. Members of the jury, consider your verdict."

We all stood as he left the court. No sooner was he gone than a tremendous noise broke out, everybody chattering and expounding their own views on the case. The heat and stench were by this time almost unbearable, and Mrs. Firth, looking pale, leaned her head against her husband's shoulder. He put his arm about her to support her.

"You had better leave the court, Meg," said Mr. Sykes. "This is too much for you."

"I prefer to remain, Father," said Mrs. Firth faintly.

"You were splendid, Tom," said Harry in my ear, leaning forward from the bench behind us.

"We had better await the verdict before distributing commendations," said Mr. Sykes.

"Why should we?" objected Harry. "I think Tom was splendid."

"Harry," said Sir Henry warningly.

Mr. Sykes flipped his thumbnails in a huff. I felt a warm little hand in mine; it was Gracie's. She had too much sense to contradict her grandfather in words, but her eyes spoke her agreement with Harry silently.

At last, in about half an hour, the jury returned, and the judge was once again installed, looking cooler, more elegant and more sardonic than ever. The accused were brought up from below and placed at the bar; Hollas was white as a sheet and trembling, Jeremy was so collapsed in face and form that he was hardly recognizable, the peddler held himself upright and looked jolly. The suspense was hardly to be borne as the clerk called out the jury's names, each answering "Here" and standing.

"Gentlemen, are you agreed upon your verdict?" said the clerk.

They all said: "Yes."

"Who shall speak for you?"

"Our foreman," they said, and they all sat down save one very respectable-looking middle-aged man in a bagwig.

"Jeremy Oldfield," said the clerk, "hold up your hand."

Jeremy gazed at him vacantly, and there was an awkward

pause, till the peddler suddenly seized his arm and held it aloft.

"Look upon the prisoner," chanted the clerk. "How say you? Is Jeremy Oldfield guilty of the felony of which he stands indicted, or not guilty?"

"Guilty," said the foreman.

"And so say you all?"

"Yes."

A murmur of satisfaction ran through the court, and the same murmur arose when George Hollas, too, was pronounced guilty. For myself I waited with almost unbearable longing to hear the verdict on the peddler, for it seemed to me that he was the originator of it all, the killing and robbing of my father, the stealing and selling of the cloth.

"Anthony Dyce, hold up your hand."

The peddler shot up his hand, and looked around him smiling as if to receive applause. The court fell very silent.

"Look upon the prisoner. How say you? Is Anthony Dyce guilty of the felony of which he stands indicted, or not guilty?"

"Guilty!" cried the foreman.

There was vehemence in his tone, and the sudden great roar of the spectators showed how cordially they agreed with him. It was some minutes before the clerk and the officers could restore order. For myself, meanwhile, I was so carried away by rejoicing and relief, that I did not take note of the proceedings until suddenly there was a great hush, and in the midst the judge's clear cool voice saying:

"The judgment of the law is this: that you, and each of you, go from hence to the place from whence you came, and from thence to the place of execution, where you shall be severally hanged by the neck till you be severally and respectively dead: and the Lord have mercy on your souls."

Then the trial was over. The judge went out, officers took

the prisoners below, and everybody seemed to rush upon me, shake my hand, pat my shoulder, shout congratulations in my face, till I was quite pushed about and hot and breathless, and my new necktie torn. But in spite of all the smiling faces about me I was not happy. Jeremy and Hollas were low, mean, cruel fellows, and the peddler was a calculating villain; yet that they should die because of my evidence was a trouble to me.

"Must they be hanged, sir?" I gasped out to the sergeant across the hurly-burly.

"Are you in any doubt that they are guilty?" said he with a sharp look.

"No. I saw Jeremy and the peddler taking the cloth off the tenters."

"Those who do not wish to be hanged should not commit felonies," said he. "It is the law."

With this I tried to be content. And so, all of us from Barseland except myself talking at the top of our voices, we came out of the castle into the cold November air. It was dark, but the torches at the door flared brightly. We all paused a moment to collect ourselves, and Mrs. Firth made Gracie put on her cloak.

"Now, my boy," said Mr. Sykes to me in a surprisingly affable tone: "If I had not hired your father to come and weave for me, he would not have come to Yorkshire, and might be alive today. Is not that so?"

"That is so, sir," said I.

"Therefore, I feel a certain responsibility for you," said he. This comes a little late, thought I bitterly, but I said nothing.

"So I am quite willing to take you into Clough End as an apprentice," said Mr. Sykes in his stateliest, most condescending tone.

I was so struck with consternation at the thought that I

could only falter pleadingly: "Mr. Firth!" At the same moment Gracie said: "Father!" and Harry cried: "He only wants you because you are famous now!" "Harry," said Sir Henry warningly.

"Well, Stephen?" said Mr. Sykes. (He managed to sound pompous and overbearing in these two words alone.)

Mr. Firth cleared his throat.

"With all respect, sir," he said in a firm, plain tone: "That cannot be. Tom is my apprentice, indentured to me for seven years."

"The indentures could be broken. Meg, you may perhaps change your husband's mind for me," said Mr. Sykes.

It was a command, though indirectly expressed, and my heart sank low.

"Father," said Mrs. Firth in a trembling tone: "We cannot part with Tom. He has become like a son to us, and Upper High Royd is his home."

I stooped and kissed her hand.

Epilogue

YESTERDAY, it being Saturday, I was in Halifax with Mr. Firth—I always go to market with him nowadays. We had sold our two pieces well in the Cloth Hall—for the Upper High Royd blue had gained some celebrity from the trial—and felt free to stroll around the town and see anything which might be going on. So when we saw something of a crowd at the door of an inn, and folk running in that direction, we, too, walked over.

A coach stood there with its shafts down, and an officer of the law waited impatiently by the door while the ostler brought out a relay of horses. Somebody cried out: "Tom Leigh!" We pushed nearer, and to my surprise there in the coach were the three prisoners, Jeremy, Hollas and the peddler. It was the peddler—of course, thought I—that had called me. He was leaning his hands on the window ledge: his wrists were in chains, but he was smiling.

"Good morning, Tom Leigh," said he. "I see your arm is whole again."

"I thought you were dead a week since," said Mr. Firth bluntly.

"Our sentences were commuted. We were recommended as fit objects for the royal mercy, and His Majesty graciously extended it to us."

"Upon condition of transportation," said Hollas, putting out his head.

"Are you to be transported, then?" asked my master.

"Aye, to Maryland in America. We are on our way to Liverpool now to board ship."

"Your wife, Hollas, is to remain mistress of Barseland poorhouse," Mr. Firth told him. "And Mr. Gledhill has arranged with your cousin to send regular supplies of mutton. Why did you ever take to selling stolen goods, you silly fellow?"

Hollas growled, and withdrew his head. Maryland would be the loser by his sullen presence, I thought.

"Why are you not wearing your father's watch, Tom?" minced the peddler. "I am sure that admirable Sir Henry returned it to you."

"I leave it safe at home when I come to market for fear of pickpockets," said I.

"Wise, very wise. Hearkee, Tom," went on the peddler quickly, as the fresh horses were backed into the shafts. "I have wished to see thee and tell thee the tale straight. It was I, as thou thought, who called out to thy father, and who took his watch and guineas, but believe me, Tom, I did not mean to kill him."

"Only to stun and rob him," said I.

"That is so," said the peddler calmly. "I am a scoundrel, Tom, as thou hast well perceived. But an entertaining scoundrel. Is it not so?"

"I do not find scoundrels entertaining," I said. "They cause too much grief."

"I pulled thee and thy father out of the beck, both. It was Jeremy who struck you on the head."

"I give you thanks for that," I said. "But to speak truth, I do not know which of you I dislike most, though I think it is you."

"Jeremy," cried the peddler with a grin, "come speak to your old friend Tom Leigh."

There was a clanking of chains, and a heavy rumbling as

of an iron ball attached to his ankle, and Jeremy appeared at the window. He looked pale, thin and wretched.

"What cheer, Jeremy!" said Mr. Firth kindly. "Take heart, man! They will need good weavers in Maryland, choose how. Keep away from Dyce here and you may yet do well."

"Aye, keep away from Dyce," I said.

"Wish us luck, Tom," said the peddler with a look of mischief.

"Well—I wish you luck," I said.

The driver mounted the box, the law officer climbed in beside his prisoners, and amid the hootings and execrations of the crowd, the coach drove away out of my life.

About the Author

PHYLLIS BENTLEY has had a successful career as a writer since 1928, with over fifteen novels and several short stories and works of nonfiction published here and in England. Her autobiography, *O Dreams, O Destinations*, appeared in 1962. "Almost the whole of my work," she says, "presents a large and I hope vivid picture of life in my native West Riding of Yorkshire, from the sixteenth century to the present day. THE ADVENTURES OF TOM LEIGH (her first novel for children) covers an important part of that picture."

Miss Bentley attended Cheltenham Ladies' College, took her B.A. at London University, and in 1949 received an honorary Doctor of Literature degree from the University of Leeds. Her home is a seventeenth-century clothier's house in Yorkshire, very much like the farmhouse of the Firths, with a view of the Pennine scenery from her study window. When she is not writing, Miss Bentley pursues her favorite hobby, amateur dramatics. She is president of the Halifax Thespians, a Little Theater group which runs a studio for teen-agers, designs its own scenery, and makes its own costumes.